Also by Lance C Wilson

TEARS OVER THE KIMBERLEYS
THE CHILDREN OF KIMBERLEY COTTAGE
DARE TO LIVE THE DREAM
DARK SIDE OF THE ROCK

THE LAIRD OF BRAIDWOOD

SHORT STORIES:
BILLY OF THE NORTH
MY FIELD OF DREAMS

THE STONE PEOPLE

ANOTHER FAST-MOVING NOVEL BY

BESTSELLING OUTBACK AUTHOR

Lance C Wilson

KIMBERLEY

cottage publishing

National Library of Australia Cataloguing-in-Publication entry

Author: Wilson, Lance C., 1945- author.

Title: The stone people / Lance C Wilson ;
Moira Horrocks, editor.

ISBN: 9780977550555 (paperback)

Subjects: Country life--Australia--Fiction.
Aboriginal Australians--Fiction.

Other Authors/Contributors:
Horrocks, Moira, editor.

A823.4

Edited by Moira Horrocks
ebook and cover design Jo Grant

This is for three wonderful women
who make my books possible:
my wife Cynthia, Jo Grant and
Moira Horrocks.

ACKNOWLEDGEMENTS

Special thanks to my graphic designer and confidante Jo Grant, who works long hours putting my books together; a true inspiration. Special thanks to my editor Moira Horrocks who turns my spelling mistakes and shocking grammar, into books.

Again, my sincere gratitude to the many outlets all over Australia for stocking my books. The stunning book cover is attributed to Alan Jennison, a talented photographer, who joined us in Arnhem Land in 2013, and delighted hundreds with his superb wildlife photography.

A special thank you to my wife Cynthia, not only for all her hard work and for cooking delicious buffalo roasts for our many guests in Arnhem Land, but for providing me with endless cups of coffee when I am writing. Thank you.

Lastly, sincere thanks to all my readers who send me the most inspiring emails; they bring so much joy to an author.

Once again, thank you to everyone and I do hope you enjoy this story.

FOREWORD

I do hope you enjoy this novel. Although fiction, it enters the realm of a subject most of the populace are uninformed of or are even aware, that such peoples existed in ancient Australia.

Between the 1940s and the 1960s, pygmies lived in North Queensland. According to records in the anthropological textbooks at that time, they had come in "from the wild of the tropical rainforests to live in missions in the region". Despite photographs of the pygmies confirming their existence and the Bradshaw rock paintings (Gwion Gwion) – *where are they now?*

Two reasons for their disappearance have been recorded; a heated debate within the anthropological academic discipline had the view "that there was nothing remarkable" about the pygmies and secondly, the radical Aboriginal political movement of the 1960s, which "found the existence of a pygmy people an inconvenient counter-example to one of its central doctrines". The latter reason resulted in the air-brushing of history to suit the needs of this particular draconian movement. So much of our past history of migration and the different waves of early migration are being destroyed in order to preserve the political dogma of the Aboriginal activists and their white sympathisers.

The Escarpment Country is one of the most isolated and unexplored regions in the world today. The Debil Debil (devil-devil) or Dreaming country was a part of Australia even the tribes of Arnhem Land never entered. The Delyangs – described as a backward, underdeveloped tribe in comparison to other coastal and inland tribes – lived on the edge of the escarpment near Havelock Falls and described the Stone People as "living in holes like lizards".

Sadly, in the early part of the century, European prospectors who entered the southern area of the Escarpment Country shot many of these primitive and shy people, rendering them even more timid and terrified as a result of these encounters with outsiders and their modern firearms.

It may be worthy to note that according to a census conducted in 1947, all the tribes that inhabited the eastern part of Arnhem Land amounted to less than 1,400 tribal Aboriginals. During the war years in Darwin, many of the tribal members who had drifted in from all over Arnhem Land, succumbed to the convenient lifestyle offered in Darwin. This was the beginning of the end of their traditional way of life.

Few redeeming passages exist of our history on our treatment of Aboriginals. This story is not unusual in its depiction of racism and appalling treatment of those who were non-whites. But as an historian, I contend this does not allow for the whitewashing of early migration to Australia over the millennia. If you are interested in one of the most enthralling accounts of early Arnhem Land, please read

Whispering Wind: Adventures in Arnhem Land by Syd Kyle-Little, an early Patrol Officer for the Australian Native Affairs Branch in Darwin. He recounts his patrols (1946 and 1950) through this rugged and hostile country on horseback, foot and canoe with two trusted Aboriginal scouts (trackers).

Syd Kyle-Little was one of the many unsung heroes of early Australia – a man who had a special rapport with Indigenous Australia and a true benefactor who fought valiantly to stop the warring factions from fighting with the deadly shovel-nosed spears over vast areas of early Arnhem Land. He was a unique individual who sadly passed away in 2012 while I was writing this novel. The founder of Maningrida, he was buried with full Aboriginal honours between his two trusted Indigenous trackers.

Hopefully, one day, history will recognise Syd Kyle-Little, who warned of the possible destruction of Indigenous Australia if they left their tribal lands and succumbed to the alcohol, tobacco and other vices of "white" Australia.

Unfortunately, his premonitions proved him right and so much of our ancient culture has been swallowed up in the western greed for power and money. My own ancestor, Thomas Braidwood Wilson, was the first white man to record the didgeridoo and the languages of the northern tribes which are fully documented in his book *Narrative of a Voyage Round the World*. He also forewarned of the problems facing Indigenous Australians from white settlement.

ONE

Priscilla Ashton-Jones sat alone in her late father's office, slowly gazing at a lifetime's work. Like herself, he had been a doctor of anthropology. She exhaled a stream of smoke into the air and immediately cursed herself for her weakness; her late father had been a smoker and his beloved pipe still lay in the tray on the desk. With the demise of her father, Priscilla was now the sole remaining member of her family. They had been very close. Decades before, a younger brother had been killed in a car accident and her mother, who had never recovered, literally drank herself to death.

Priscilla had followed in her late father's footsteps and after graduation, had obtained a job in England, only to return a few months later to nurse her sick father. It had been heart-wrenching to watch him succumb to lung cancer and at his funeral; she swore to kick the habit but was finding it harder than she had ever anticipated.

Having never married – each relationship seemed to falter over a short period of time – and now approaching fifty; she begrudgingly accepted that a permanent relationship was highly unlikely. Sighing, she looked again at the pile of papers on the desk before her and shaking her head, picked up the first file placed neatly on her right. Opening it, she began to read and within minutes, was enthralled at its contents.

Her father had left his entire estate to Priscilla and along with the proceeds of a house sale in London, now found herself rather well off. She had decided to live in the family home for the time being at least. Having arrived at an impasse in her life, she had no immediate plans but to sort and file her father's life work and maybe, at a later stage, donate it to someone of authority who might find his research beneficial. However, being fully aware of the political climate, she was sure that under these conditions, what lay in front of her would most certainly interest anyone.

Priscilla knew that her father had had great interest in the Bradshaw paintings of Western Australia. Up until the early seventies, it had been well documented that local Aboriginals had recorded them as being "not of their time and that the cave paintings distributed right throughout the Kimberley as being painted by birds with bleeding beaks". In previous years, access to these paintings had been severely restricted and if their presence had been raised, the modern mantra would have been that they had been painted by "our ancestors".

Priscilla's father had in fact, uncovered attempts to paint over some of the paintings and restrict academic access. In his opinion, it was patently obvious by these paintings, that the people who had painted these figures had been a distinctly *different* race to the present day population of Aboriginals.

Another unexplained mystery that he spent much time

researching, was the 5,000-year-old Egyptian hieroglyphs found in New South Wales. *Did the ancient Egyptians once colonise ancient Australia or simply become shipwrecked off the coast?* Some of the glyphs relate to the time just after the reign of King Khufu, the alleged builder of the Great Pyramid.

The Gympie Pyramid in Queensland is thought by some to have been constructed by unknown ancient civilisations, possibly early European immigrants. Amateur speculation exists that it was the work of an Italian farmer, but disagreement still rages as to the exact time of construction.

His other interest had been the pygmies of Queensland, now unfortunately extinct and certainly extinct from any authorities' records. Only those few who dared to prove their existence with old photos of a group taken in a rainforest behind Cairns in 1890, proves they ever existed.

But what truly captivated Priscilla was reading the research over his last few years of life into the existence of the Stone People of Arnhem Land. Her father had personally visited a remote coastal community and spoken to an elderly Aboriginal who had told him of a contact he had had with the "little people" only fifteen years previously. The elderly Aboriginal had described them as "little fellas" or Stone People, of the high and remote Escarpment Country which he called Debil Debil country. He recounted that they were, "different to us people, we have nothing to do with them, they bad people, kill us".

Priscilla was intrigued as she appreciated how her father had battled against the entrenched mantra that "all Aboriginals belonged to the same grouping". His notes went on to state that research indicated that several waves of migration *had* occurred by different groups but that the subject had been bitterly opposed. Her father had often quoted what a travesty it was that research – especially now with DNA sampling – had been obstructed. Even in Tasmania, the remains that had been returned had been burned to prevent any research, even though no evidence had been uncovered that such a practice had actually occurred.

Upon reading the file, Priscilla felt deeply that perhaps there *was* a way to validate her father's theory, if only she were able to locate members of this group and get blood samples for DNA purposes. She began to gather all the information her father had collected, including reading the most fascinating account of Syd Kyle-Little, who had explored the region and wrote a book called *Whispering Wind*; he had actually met the Stone People in an antagonistic meeting in the 1950s. This information, coupled with her father's meeting with an Aboriginal elder in Arnhem Land, gave her a glimmer of hope – of the possibility that some may *still exist* in this most remote region of Australia.

Priscilla found an early map that showed the Gungurgone region discovered in the Cooktown Museum by her father; all later maps excluded it. Further notes showed that the coastal Aboriginal did not trade or interact with the Stone People but feared them. It appeared that they deliberately kept well away from them and as the older coastal Aboriginals told her late father, "Them little ones, they kill us for sure".

Priscilla continued to read the account her father – after much probing – had obtained from an elder in a remote camp. The elder and his mate, who had been with him had died. It appeared they had been hunting redskins or bush cattle; pure shorthorn that had gone wild decades before and that now, along with buffalo and wild pigs, covered the region. The two men described how they had been standing next to a wymaitpirr or billabong with his friend on his right. Glancing behind his friend, he had spotted a "little fella" or bush Aboriginal stalking him, and immediately fired a shot and scared him off.

Armed with all these positive remnants, Priscilla felt sure that with modern science, her beloved father's life-long theory could be substantiated to disprove the politically correct version of history.

Over the next few days, with a newfound sense of the course she must take, Priscilla carefully documented and read any available information on the area. This included all the old reports of early explorers her father had collected over the decades. She knew that she would have to obtain a permit from the authorities to enter Aboriginal land but realised that somehow, she would have to find a way to circumnavigate such a request and enter legally, but without raising suspicion. Many of the reports she read showed the area she wished to explore as wild, and even today, large sections have never been visited by a "white" person, even in the early part of Australia's history. Those who lived there led, in most cases, a harsh existence.

Because of her experience researching European history and various migration patterns, Priscilla was well aware of the brutal and warlike lifestyles that existed in many countries of the world. However, the reports before her also showed that pre-European settlement of Australia did not give the average Indigenous Australian the utopian life ordinary Australians are led to believe.

One report on the practice of men to stop women running off was particularly sickening. It was written by Stuart Love ARSM who led a party into the Walker River area in 1910.

One entry on the 9th of August simply read:

This afternoon, an old black fellow and three young gins (girls) entered the camp with several children. They came from the North to our camp. The old fellow had a fine axe head mounted as a tomahawk. He himself though old, was a pretty good specimen of Aboriginal but the gins were all terribly mutilated and presented a most revolting and disgusting spectacle. One had both her feet burned off to the ankles; paper bark was bound round the stumps and she was just able to walk with great pain on these improvised wooden legs, the burns being only partly healed. One of her hands was burnt off to the wrist while the nerves and sinews of the other were so destroyed and contracted that the fingers were closed over the palm. The other two gins were badly burned but the most gruesome sight of all was a piccaninny covered with burns and sores and dirt with infinite flies. It nearly made us all sick and I shall not describe this most unpleasant spectacle further. The party had, as well, come across a deceased male whose body lay high on a wooden frame and underneath it; a gin had been speared to "assist" her master into the "afterlife".

Syd Kyle-Little's deep empathy with the Aboriginals fascinated Priscilla. As an Aboriginal affairs patrol officer, he was charged with the unenviable task of stopping tribal warfare; an ongoing problem in the 40s and 50s. All his great knowledge and advice was completely ignored. For example, there had been a young couple who had run exhausted into his camp. It appeared that the young gin was "promised" and had run off with her lover. They were being chased by a group of men, armed with shovel-nosed spears and Kyle-Little gave the couple protection while the pursuers camped nearby.

Losing nerve during the night, the couple fled. It wasn't long before the young man was found full of spears, the girl had been raped by the pursuing mob and thrown into a river with the crocodiles.

As Priscilla proceeded with her research, she and her late father both suspected that yes, all humanity is prone to barbaric acts but glossing over history to pursue a supposed great injustice is blight on any free-thinking and open society.

Now more than ever, her determination to explore the Escarpment Area and try and locate any surviving Stone People became an obsession. Days turned into weeks.

Frustration engulfed her as she knew that by using her family name, with its reputation of seeking the truth, her chances of obtaining a permit to enter Indigenous land could possibly be thwarted.

One of her father's lecture papers had been rejected outright. It was a lecture regarding Indigenous Australia and it only further underlined her father's passion on the subject that was indeed borne out of frustration and bitterness on what had indeed happened over the last few decades. Despite feeling jaded, she read his lecture over and over.

It read:

Australia has become a land of two distinct nations, each with its own flag and laws; on one side we have white Australia open to everyone from both nations and on the other, we must have a permit to enter.

About twenty one percent of the land mass is owned by Indigenous Australia subject to, in many cases, their own laws. Indigenous Australia equates to the twentieth largest nation on earth, with some of the richest and most fertile country in the world, along with enormous resources of mineral wealth. Approximately five hundred and fifty thousand people claim to be Aboriginal or of Aboriginal descent, no DNA or any other form of verification is requested; you simply associate and register yourself as Aboriginal. Although it is hard to obtain correct figures, the white nation contributes 1.3 million dollars in taxes to sustain Aboriginal

Australia per person for welfare: housing, health, roads, power stations, education and programs, which alone cost 100 thousand dollars per person. On top of this, Indigenous Australia collects, in mining royalties, 200 million dollars and in leases for national parks, tourist spots etc., another hefty figure in the millions. Recently, a female, claiming to be of Aboriginal descent, sued a well-known broadcaster for supposedly racist comments. She had been employed in the industry for years on a high salary – some background checks found out her father was an African American. We have created a nation that is so ensconced in unreal expectations and by basing an entire race of people to be absolutely reliant on their benefactors, we have done them a great injustice. The mantra is more education and jobs; yet go to any community and all the workers are European, giving them an expensive education. Few, if any, proceed past this point but simply collect welfare and continue the cycle. Until we can face the truth and make realistic decisions, the cycle will continue; drugs, alcohol and child molestation will increase. When we replace the scream "racist" with "realist", we might then be able to effect change, but to continue is surely suicidal and unsustainable.

History has been manipulated to a "politically correct" version. Research has proved that several waves of different cultures and races made the journey from Asia and I would suggest that if history teaches us any lessons, we, who populate this nation now, may be replaced one day, by a superior group or nation of people.

Priscilla placed the speech back in the folder. It went on to describe the different waves of humans inhabiting Australia. Research shows that Negrito populations (possible ancestors of Aboriginal Australians and Papuans of New Guinea), have at times swept into mainland Australia but were subsequently displaced, as elsewhere in the world, by stronger and bigger migrations.

Priscilla was even more determined to at least mount an expedition into Arnhem Land and explore the region west of the Walker River for any signs of the Stone People. All she needed was some way of gaining access to the region and someone who had knowledge of the district.

Her musings became a reality when one evening, she received an unexpected visitor – Dee Fuller, an American she had met in London. Dee was a fellow anthropologist and keen hunter, who often visited Africa. He was a most likeable fellow and they had had many a drinking session in London.

'My dear Priscilla, you look absolutely crap!' announced Dee stepping back and throwing his arms wide open.

Priscilla was so glad to see an old friend that she threw herself at him.

'Oh Dee, I'm *so glad* to see you! Since Dad's death, I must admit to having become somewhat of a recluse.'

'My dear friend,' Dee laughed, 'put on some glad rags and let's hit the town – show me Sydney's delights!'

'Dee, if you don't mind, I've been a bit down. Can we stay home? There's something important I need to discuss and *you* are that friend. I trust you completely and boy, have you arrived at a watershed in my life,' Priscilla replied breathlessly.

Priscilla escorted Dee into her father's study and as soon as she had him seated with a drink in his hand, explained her predicament. She did not hesitate in asking him to accompany her on the expedition; *if* they obtained a guide and permit.

Dee smiled, 'Well old girl, it appears I *have* come at the right time. I've hunted buffalo in that very area and know a man, Simon Black, who happens to have a safari camp there.'

Priscilla stood up and walked around the room. It all seemed so simple. She was frustrated with herself for not having thought outside the square.

'Really Dee, it would be that simple?' she asked.

'Priscilla my lovely friend, it's a splendid idea and there's no better person than myself to guide you there. I've been to that part but never as far inland as the Escarpment Area. In addition old girl, after a relationship break-up I need some adventure, some diversion. Strangely enough I *have* heard rumours of the Stone People but nothing concrete,' replied Dee seriously.

'Dee, it's a very long shot that they *do* still exist but hope springs eternal. When can you come with me or as you've already been there, when is the best time to go?'

Dee held his chin in his hand and frowned, 'Well, now actually, and as the shooting season is nearly over, maybe I can persuade Simon to take us at the end of the month. I'll phone his wife in Darwin and she'll get a message to him. He used to phone her each night on the satellite phone.'

Dee strolled to the phone and having dialled the number, turned to an excited Priscilla and grinning said, 'Pack some bags old girl oh and um, do you own a rifle?'

Frowning, and with hands on hips, Priscilla replied, 'Why on earth do I need a rifle for heaven's sake Dee?'

Dee smirked and replied, 'How can you go on a buffalo shoot without a bloody rifle dear woman?'

TWO

Simon Black sat by the crackling fire, a heavy, gulf fog rolled over the land making visibility tricky. Sipping his coffee, he listened to the world news on his shortwave radio, a practice he carried out every morning.

A veteran safari operator for twenty-five years, he had seen the good times and the bad, and this season had been his worst; the high dollar and world financial situation had slowed his customers – mainly from America – to a virtual trickle.

Today he would pick up his last customer for the season and then pack up and return to Darwin until the following season; unsure what the future held. As was his usual custom at this time of day, finishing his coffee, he continued with his daily routine and walked slowly into the lodge situated on the bank of the Walker River. Gazing below, he watched as a crocodile lazily made his way up the river, a scene often repeated but one that he never tired of watching. He was in awe of these ancient creatures; one of the greatest survivors in the animal world. Locating his satellite phone he walked a short distance to a relatively clear spot amongst the trees and gaining a signal, dialled his home number.

His wife, Jane, informed him that their last customers would be landing at a nearby airstrip at the agreed time, providing the fog lifted. If it didn't, as was the case, she would phone him and relay the delayed time of arrival. Jane then told him that a well-known former client, Dee Fuller, had rung and requested a late hunt after his present clients had departed. In actual fact, Dee had asked that if not too inconvenient for Simon, he and a female friend would arrive on the plane coming to collect his next clients.

Jane told Simon that she'd already accepted as it had been a quiet season and they liked Dee Fuller. He had been a great client and indeed had become a good friend. Simon smiled as he ended the conversation. Fuller was outgoing and the pair had formed an amicable relationship. Simon Black looked forward to the visit of his old friend, and the money would be handy too.

With a sudden spring in his step, Simon checked the vehicle before heading the ten kilometres to pick up the new clients – no mechanics out here – all breakdowns had to be repaired on site as it was a two-day drive through rough terrain back to "civilisation". Even the short trip to the airstrip was what most four-wheel drive enthusiasts would describe as a challenge. Starting the Toyota Land Cruiser, he glanced swiftly at the camp. This was the first time in two years he had used his main camp; it had been inundated by flood waters both preceding wet seasons and he'd only recently reopened it. It had been a difficult task but he was glad to be operating again from his own lodge.

For two seasons he had used two houses some distance away that had been built for their Indigenous owners who had never taken up residence. In fact, the airstrip he now journeyed to had been built close to a settlement that had long been abandoned by the Aboriginal owners. The airstrip was going to be used for emergency situations for the Aboriginal inhabitants but for now, he was the sole user of the facility.

After arriving at the airstrip, Simon then, in his usual manner, entered the abandoned village and used the still operational phone to make several business calls. He was still on the phone when he heard the drone of an aircraft approaching. Finishing his call, he made his way to the airstrip in time to see the small plane, owned by an Aboriginal corporation, on its final approach. As it was about to land, he heard the engine of the aircraft rise quickly to full power as it suddenly climbed to go around and make another approach. It was only then that Simon noticed a small herd of buffalo which had originally been in the swamp but had now made their way onto the northern end of the runway. Wisely, the experienced pilot had decided to make another approach and not chance an unnerved buffalo causing an accident!

Alighting from the aircraft, his two clients, husband and wife team, smiled as Simon approached to welcome them. They were chatting incessantly about the "near miss" they had just had and praised the skills of their young pilot and his quick thinking. John and Betty Voss from Texas had travelled the world following their passion of big-game hunting. Simon had been highly recommended by friends as having one of the biggest and most prolific numbers of big buffalo in the Northern Territory.

His clients would be in his care for five days and wanted a prize set of buffalo horns each, plus, if possible and time permitting, a boar each; the area was well known for its three hundred kilogram wild boars.

Arriving back at camp, the trio enjoyed morning tea before sighting the rifles they had brought with them. Simon was relieved to learn that they were efficient shots, hitting the bulls-eye on three occasions. Wounded buffalo can be extremely dangerous and while a veteran at the game, he detested clients wounding the magnificent beasts. Simon was always anxious for a good, clean shot and quick death for the chosen beast.

John and Betty, having only just arrived, were eager to start their hunting expedition. Simon knew of a burnt area with fresh grass some thirty kilometres away and they set off scouring the landscape for a trophy animal.

They saw several herds of buffalo and several good-sized bulls and although John and Betty seemed keen to shoot rather large-looking specimens, Simon begged them to err on the side of caution. He advised them that, having spent a great deal of money in getting there, reacting prematurely would not give them value for their money, as he was certain that a finer specimen could be located in areas where he knew they existed. They stopped for photos of wild dingoes and a herd of wild cattle that stampeded as they approached; shorthorn cattle that had escaped from the early settlers and spread all over Eastern Arnhem Land and possibly the purest bloodlines of shorthorns left in the world, due to their isolation.

In this area of Arnhem Land, at the head of the Walker River and within sight of the Escarpment Country, the vegetation is rather thick and only open spaces afford decent views and photos of wild buffalo. Breaking into open wetlands at the mouth of the Walker River, Betty and John asked Simon to stop, and grabbing their cameras, alighted from the vehicle hurriedly.

'Absolutely amazing!' exclaimed Betty. 'It's unbelievable that a vista like this still exists in the world.'

Before them, thousands of birds of all shapes, sizes and colours twirled in the air and waded in the vast expanse of open wetlands. Even Simon, who was so used to the vision, had to admit it was scenes like these that had continually pulled him back to the isolation and hard life of a remote safari operator.

In the distance, buffalo grazed on the open plains but as darkness began to flood the land, Simon was anxious to start the return journey. Operating the camp on his own, he still had the evening meal to prepare for his clients. He'd employed an older couple to assist in the running of the camp for the season but unfortunately they had left early in the week because of health problems. He didn't blame them because here in the isolation of Arnhem Land, one's health was paramount. Simon now found himself doing myriad jobs running a successful safari lodge as well as guiding clients who expected first-class service and in most cases, his undivided attention.

Simon was tired and looking forward to returning to civilised life and family. It was hard going maintaining an efficient camp in such isolation; even obtaining supplies from Katherine was a four-day journey over mostly hard and unforgiving country with wide and deep river crossings. Simon was relieved his clients appeared easy to get along with; both experienced hunters, they seemed to understand the effort that was required to keep such an enterprise going in such trying circumstances.

By the time the three of them had made the arduous journey back to the lodge, all were relieved to have a refreshing shower and a few cold drinks around the blazing fire, whilst Simon cooked a refreshing meal of barramundi, a fish that was prolific in the Walker River.

It wasn't long before Betty and John started to yawn and feel the effects of a long and tiring day. The delicious fish meal washed down by a bottle of red wine was the perfect ending to their first day. They excused themselves and made their way to the luxurious tent situated a short distance on the bank of the river, stopping only to listen to the haunting call of a night bird and the barking of crocodiles in the river below.

Simon cleared the table, washed the dishes and then set the table for breakfast. Balancing dishes and cutlery, he picked up the satellite phone and made his usual check-in to Jane. She had nothing much to report and after a chat, bid his two children goodnight and turned in himself.

Deep in sleep, Simon was suddenly woken by the sound of buffalo walking through the campsite. He turned over and ignored them; it had been a tiring day. There had been occasions in the past when the marauding animals had caused him grief and nearly a calamity.

On that occasion, a bull had somehow managed to get his horns entangled in the tent stays and had bolted, pulling the startled inhabitants some distance before breaking the stay ropes and releasing the terrified occupants of the tent! As Simon recollected the traumatic ordeal, he could not help but smile and went back to sleep.

In this isolated part of the world, with its millions of acres of unspoiled beauty and wild uncharted country, nothing was unexpected. The coastal Aborigines had always lived on the coast or river systems and had studiously avoided the interior as they were terrified of the "little fellas", as Simon had often heard them described. Through his own father's experience in the interior and the stories of his Aboriginal friends, he too knew a lot of history on the little people, commonly known as, the Stone People.

Waking up refreshed, as the first of the sun's rays crawled eerily across the landscape through dense fog – a usual occurrence here inland on the Gulf of Carpentaria – Simon rose and lit the fire to heat water for his morning coffee. While waiting for the water to boil, he listened on his shortwave to the ABC news.

Many mornings, he felt almost sorry to hear the usual spin and lies of politicians and tens of thousands of bureaucrats who seemed unable to deliver the most basic of government responsibilities without cost blowouts, gross mismanagement and incompetence. Shaking his head, he turned off the radio as John and Betty joined him and poured a cup of steaming coffee; the only three humans for hundreds of kilometres.

John spoke to Simon as he sipped the welcome brew, 'I saw you listening to the news Simon, anything of importance?'

Shaking his head from side to side, Simon answered sarcastically, 'Only the same incompetence and spin from our supposed people whom we vote in to undertake we, the people's wishes.'

John threw back his head and roared with laughter. 'My dear man, your country can be no worse than our debt-ridden, once great country; absolutely destroyed by those we vote in and trust to run our nation. They tell us they're gonna fix it, yet like your lot, they're the ones who caused the problem in the first place!'

Simon smiled, 'Oh well, not much we can do about it and the younger set seem not to care. Let's have breakfast and get you a really nice trophy buffalo to take home.'

Betty laughed, 'Come on you two, let's forget all this morbid talk about politicians and let Simon live up to his high reputation as the best outfitter in Australia.'

After a hearty breakfast, everyone piled into the Land Cruiser with an esky full of food and water; essential in this remote location where help could be days away. By mid-morning, they had travelled thirty kilometres through rough and treacherous country and despite many buffalo and wild pigs – nothing was of outstanding trophy size. Pulling up at the edge of an escarpment, Simon invited his guests to leave the vehicle. Relieved at the opportunity to stretch their legs, John and Betty eagerly complied. Walking a short distance, Simon pointed to an enormous sinkhole as big as a football field. John and Betty gasped at the sight.

'Not many white people have seen that or are even aware of its existence,' Simon told them.

'Truly astonishing,' whispered Betty as she walked as close as she dared towards its edge.

'How deep is it Simon, do you know?' asked John.

Picking up a decent-sized stone, Simon hurled it into the abyss. The silence hung heavily over the sinkhole and after what seemed an eternity, they eventually heard the stone hit faintly below.

'I wonder what's in a sinkhole like that. What happens down there over time?' thought Betty out loud.

'No one, to my knowledge, has ever been to the bottom, so the answer to that question, if one knew, would be very interesting,' Simon replied.

The sun was now climbing and the day warming up as they continued to drive south. They encountered wild horses and plenty of buffalo and the odd drove of wild oxen that immediately took flight upon seeing or sensing their presence. No prize buffalo bull was sighted.

At lunchtime, they stopped at the entrance to an enormous escarpment. For centuries, a river running through it had cut a deep stream into the mountain range. With lunch over, Simon proudly continued to show Betty and John the magic of the region that he held a concession over in a deal with the Aboriginal owners. After a short but difficult walk, Betty and John were once again enthralled and speechless at the beauty of what they saw. High up above, as if from the heavens, fell a magnificent waterfall which cascaded over sharp, dark rocks in a most spectacular fashion. It was breathtaking.

John turned to Simon and asked smiling, 'Simon, what have you next got up your sleeve? So far today, we've been privy to two outstanding examples of natural beauty in this magnificent and isolated country!'

Simon replied grinning, 'Better show you a good trophy bull! That's what you came for.'

Shouldering his rifle, Simon led his clients back to the vehicle. When with his clients in the bush, he always carried his rifle; always expect the unexpected in this part of the world.

The party stopped several times and by mid-afternoon, Simon spied a massive bull at the edge of a lagoon, now nearly dry. Climbing out from the vehicle quietly and cautiously, the three hunters stalked the beast, ensuring to remain downwind so as not to cause their target *and* the many cows and calves present, to scatter into the thick bush nearby.

Simon was grateful that the couple had good experience in their chosen sport and that their approach was professional. When within range, Simon indicated to Betty, who had been nominated as the first to shoot a trophy. Raising her rifle in one smooth action – even Simon was enthused – she sighted and squeezed the trigger. The roar of the heavy calibre rifle rattled across the landscape as the old battle-scarred bull crashed to the ground.

John and Betty were elated at the tremendous trophy horns! Simon was happy for them but knew that his hard work had only just begun, and the rest of the day and well into the night would be spent skinning and preparing the head and hide for shipping to a taxidermist in the United States.

THREE

Dee Fuller looked at Priscilla as she stepped out of the changing room of the camping store. That morning, an excited Priscilla had suggested they go into the city and buy suitable clothing for the expedition they now had only three days to prepare for.

He smiled as she paraded before him, nodding in approval. Although he had known Priscilla for many years, he had been in a steady relationship but now, given his new status, he began to view her in a different light. Dee knew too, that she had always been attracted to him but to date, in the short time he had been with her on this trip, neither had made any move towards any romance.

'You look smashing Priscilla old girl,' he beamed.

'You always were a bullshitter Dee my love,' Priscilla replied, laughing coquettishly.

The banter continued as they paid and left the store, and over a long lunch, final plans were made for their departure. Dee was uncertain as to Simon's reaction to request a hunt in the escarpment area, as he had heard that some old bulls get driven from their herds by younger, stronger animals into the high Escarpment Country.

He knew that Simon had, on one occasion, taken an

American hunter into the same area and that it had almost turned pear-shaped. The client, a crusty old ex-marine named Clint, had requested a camping trip into the Escarpment Country. Parking the vehicle at one of the many empty Aboriginal settlements on the edge of the range, he and Simon had taken off on a quad bike across the last river into semi-desert country, carrying only bare essentials to survive a few days. They camped roughly at night by sleeping on the ground.

After more than thirty kilometres, they were disappointed at the lack of game. On their third morning, with supplies running low, the rear diff of the quad disintegrated. Luckily, the quad, with help over rough or steep patches, held together; driven only by the front wheels. After two punishing days of pushing and picking their way through treacherous country with no water and temperatures reaching 40 degrees, the two men managed to return to the Land Cruiser. Clint became so dehydrated that his body cramped, and at one stage, could only walk backwards for several kilometres. This tale travelled far and wide and he was eventually nicknamed "Walk Backwards" but his tenacity and determination highlighted the grit of the tough little individual and he became a campfire legend.

Dee remembered talking to Clint, who had told him about one night when he was sleeping by a rough, old game track, he had felt the presence of something or someone. They had camped very close to a small, round fire not many days old. The drama did not end there as upon their return, the Land

Cruiser would not start and it took them hours to get it sorted. It was only their resolve and the experience of Simon that had saved the day.

When Dee relayed this story to Priscilla, emphasising the hardship and danger they would no doubt face; her response had simply been, 'Dee, that campfire was left by the Stone People. It's only fifteen years since one was shot and with this information, it's likely that some may still be around today. Come on Dee, this is a *mammoth* adventure!'

Dee simply shook his head. Since meeting up with Priscilla he was happy now to spend more time with her, and he'd always liked Simon Black, a tough, no-nonsense individual whom he had every confidence in to pull this off. Dee knew too, that Simon had had a few lean years and Priscilla was prepared to pay whatever it took to follow her dream.

Two days passed with Priscilla and Dee making final arrangements and under Dee's guidance, Priscilla eventually relented after Dee's insistence, to downsize her substantial luggage to *one* suitcase!

'Dee my friend, it appears you want me to run out of clothes and get around like Jane in the Tarzan movies!' Priscilla laughed.

'Hmm, not a bad idea, but I can tell you that of all your expeditions, this one will be the most testing and even dangerous. Once we're in the escarpment area, any chance of outside help will be almost impossible; we will be on *our own*. I have every faith in Simon, he is the most capable man to have on board with such an excursion,' Dee replied confidently.

'Well, I feel that I too must warn you Dee that what we're about to do is absolutely politically incorrect and whatever the outcome, we might be or more possibly, *will* be vilified, whatever our findings,' Priscilla warned him.

'Ah, my dear Priscilla, I read only last week that some *astute* person had explained political correctness as follows, quote:

Political correctness is a doctrine, fostered by the delusional, illogical minority, and rabidly promoted by an unscrupulous mainstream media, which holds forth the proposition that it is entirely possible to pick up a piece of shit by the clean end, unquote, Dee replied in an arrogant tone.

Priscilla roared with laughter and said, 'Dee, of all the times in my life when I needed someone like you, it is right now. Honestly, I sense that you actually don't give a stuff! I'm too old now for all that crap.'

'Precisely, Priscilla my love – am always honest. To be perfectly frank, I'm more interested in getting into your pants than worrying about any political ramifications,' Dee replied unabashed.

Priscilla turned her face away, flushed. Dee moved towards her and pushed the suitcase off the bed. He lay her down on the bed and kissed her gently and slowly, but soon his passion and desire overcame any shyness on Priscilla's behalf. Breaking from the embrace, they tore off their clothes, pieces of clothing flying around the room. They embraced again, this time naked, and Priscilla wrapped her long, lean legs around Dee as he roughly entered her. Their two bodies entwined, they were now lost in pure ecstasy, meeting each other in powerful thrusts with moans of pleasure filling the room as they climaxed together.

'God I needed that Dee!' Priscilla exclaimed panting wildly as they rolled apart.

'My dear Priscilla, not only you I can assure you. Ever since I got here, the thought of sex with you has been well and truly on my mind,' Dee replied gasping for breath.

'Well Dee, my delicious shagging mate, I have to be honest, the idea had crossed my mind too', Priscilla chuckled.

'Priscilla old love, may we have many more shags in the future,' said Dee as he rolled over and held her in his arms.

Priscilla and Dee did not leave the bed for the rest of the day. They shared a hunger for each other and it was only the next morning after several marathons did the two lovers shower and dress. No words were spoken; they had created an intimate bond which was perfectly tuned to the needs of each other. They were two outgoing people of the world; truly free spirits.

Once they were up, they then focused on closing up the house – left to Priscilla by her late father – and then called a taxi to take them to Kingsford Smith airport. There, they boarded a flight to Cairns and then onto Gove where they stayed overnight before catching the flight to the safari camp on the Walker River. There was no going back.

Arriving in Gove late that evening, they caught a taxi to

the Walkabout Hotel where they partook of a delicious meal, accompanied by a few wines. They were tired, happy and excited at the same time. Retiring to their room, they snuggled into each other's arms and soon fell asleep. Tomorrow held adventure as well as their unexpected newly formed relationship.

Simon had arranged permits for the trip and Dee and Priscilla had purposely planned to arrive a day early in order to visit the settlement of Yirrkala. They wanted to browse the Aboriginal art, produced by the locals and reputed to be of high quality.

Back at the hotel, Dee and Priscilla slept in; revelling in their new love. Priscilla mused on the possibility of settling down with Dee. Her career had seen her travel to many exotic places in the world but if she were honest with herself, she had had more than her fair share of travel and adventure. She considered that after this particular research, she should focus on a more stable and conventional lifestyle. Sadly, she had left it too late for children and with no other immediate family, sharing her life with Dee seemed particularly attractive.

It was nearly midday when they drove the short distance to the Aboriginal Community and entered the art centre. After some time browsing, they bought a small animal carving as a memento of the visit and after paying, struck up a conversation with the young lady behind the counter. They informed her that they had a safari booked on the Walker River and she obviously knew the operator, Simon Black; many of his clients visited the art gallery on his recommendation.

Just then, an elderly lady entered the store carrying two carved birds. She stood shyly waiting for the couple to leave; however, the outgoing Dee approached her and requested to look at her work. The artist was more than happy; Dee was interested in her work and the two started to chat. What happened next was so interesting, that Priscilla and Dee looked at each other in total surprise. They then questioned the lady more closely.

Dee had replied to her question as to what they were doing in Gove as most people worked for the mine, and although a few tourists did visit, it always created some interest. Dee told the lady about their safari and how they were keen to include the escarpment area west of the Walker River.

The elderly lady then said, 'That where them little people live, little fella; they bad people, them kill us, we stay away, bad country.'

Not to relay any suspicion of their intent, Dee replied, 'Are there small pygmy people in that area? I have never heard of them.'

The old lady smiled, 'Me come from Numbulwar; we coastal people, we never mix or go near that Debil Debil country.'

A sense of elation came over Priscilla and Dee as they left the store and hopped into the back of the waiting taxi. Heavy spits of rain started pounding on the red dust as they left the village for the return to Nhulunbuy, also known as Gove.

On the way back, neither spoke. The encounter and information had boosted their expectations; was there *really* a chance that evidence of the Stone People still existed in this vast and remote area and more so – *would they be lucky enough to find them?*

It was only when they were back in their hotel room and had closed the door that they looked at each other and feverishly discussed the old woman's remarks. The information had been openly given and they had no reason to doubt her sincerity. They were of the opinion that further discussion with the friendly elderly artist would have been fruitful.

Neither gave any thought to the early storm that belted down outside in torrents. They jumped into bed and rested for the afternoon and their forthcoming challenge. Their departure was early the next morning, south by charter plane to the small Walker River airstrip.

Their afternoon slumber was shattered when Dee's phone rang; slipping out from the bed he answered it.

'Hi Dee, it's Jane, how are you? Arrived safely?' she asked.

Dee knew it was Jane's responsibility to check on the clients and replied, 'Yes. Arrived yesterday, thanks Jane. How are you?'

'Fine thanks Dee but we have a problem in that the storm has made the small strip dangerous according to the pilot, so pick-up will be at Numbulwar airstrip. Regretful I know, but all the more so for Simon, as now he has a nine-hour dash to take his present clients back and pick you up,' informed Jane.

'How will Simon go with the rivers Jane? Especially the Harris?' asked Dee concerned.

'Simon believes that by morning, if we have no more rain, they will be passable. Unfortunately, the mission plane we had hired for you will not land on the Walker strip, if the young pilots from the Aboriginal airline had been free I think they would have,' answered Jane.

'Okay, we'll be at the airport at nine am Jane. Let's go for it and many thanks,' replied Dee and hung up.

Turning to Priscilla he smiled, 'Well old girl, the adventure has begun! It appears we have to fly to Numbulwar and Simon will drive us in from there; the rain has made the strip we'd been scheduled to land on, unsafe.'

'Oh well, I'm determined to make this work; sounds like we may see lots more than we originally bargained for!' replied Priscilla cheerfully.

'Bloody right there my love, and you'll certainly agree with me by the time we get to camp tomorrow night,' chuckled Dee.

Jumping back into bed, Dee grabbed hold of Priscilla who feigned alarm as he gently parted her legs. In a tight embrace, the pair made slow and sensuous love before drifting off to sleep.

FOUR

Simon Black had had a good hunt. His clients had shot and killed two fine buffalo heads with high scores and two boars; in all, a successful hunt with extremely satisfied clients.

John and Betty retired to bed and Simon, having just returned from salting the trophies down and feeling in a good mood, phoned his wife.

On receiving the news of the plane diversion he was furious. During the day, only the edge of the storm had reached them and barely wet the ground. Fires lit up the night sky to the east; burning by the Indigenous Ranger program via helicopter had begun. Jane immediately phoned the chief pilot of the plane they had hired and he was adamant he would not risk the landing at such a remote strip until the strip had dried. Jane relayed the information much to Simon's disgust. He was *not* looking forward to hours of driving when it was far from necessary, but being reliant on charter planes, he had no alternative.

Even though he was tired, he filled the vehicle ready for the trip. He had to wake his sleeping clients to inform them of the change in plan. To reach the township airstrip at Numbulwar, they would have to depart at five am.

No matter how many times Simon made the arduous trip

to Numbulwar and then onto Katherine and subsequently Darwin, the initial trip to Numbulwar was always a major challenge. This was because the track had long been neglected since it was first constructed to transport the many new homes and facilities for the proposed Indigenous population to return; a plan that never eventuated.

Although hundreds of new homes with toilet and shower facilities were constructed, along with airstrips, phone services, playgrounds, water towers and solar hot water services, everything now lay abandoned and the road in complete disrepair; millions wasted on a futile exercise. He was aware that the same scenario had taken place all over the Northern Territory and Kimberley region of West Australia and included some areas of South Australia.

Waking as usual long before daybreak, Simon checked his watch and was alarmed to read it was already ten minutes past five! He dressed hurriedly and in the darkness, woke his clients, apologising for being so late and impressing upon them that to catch the flight they would have to depart as soon as possible. Luckily their cases were packed and they suggested to Simon that they grab some food and eat on the way. Simon was impressed with their assistance, although he'd always found the Americans amicable and easy to get along with.

Before long, the Land Cruiser with the group was heading east, following the trail from the ghostly light given off by the vehicle; no backup here if any problems occurred. The track wound down to the Walker River crossing. It still flowed strongly and the trio could feel the pressure of the water as the vehicle made its way through the surging waters, then began the long climb up over a mountain range on little more than a goat track. Slowly descending the other side, Simon picked his way through a billabong, seeking new and sound footing for the vehicle; one mistake and he knew the vehicle would become seriously bogged.

Once they hit open country, they then passed through a bigger Aboriginal settlement which contained many houses and gigantic mango trees. Several buffalo bolted from one of the homes the Aboriginals used to sleep in. Crossing a small stream, the group picked up speed as the country became more open and on several occasions, buffalo, and at one stage wild horses, bolted onto the road in fright and ran for short periods in front of them.

Daylight streaked through the trees above and it soon got to the stage where Simon was navigating without the headlights. After a couple of hours they reached one of the most arduous crossings; a precipitous drop into the Harris Creek, the only way out. It then involved a short trip up the river, then a sheer climb out the other side. The average city four-wheel experts would never ever contemplate or attempt to cross it but several wet seasons had completely annihilated the original crossing.

'Are you *serious* Simon?' squeaked Betty in fear as they plunged into the river.

'Hang on folks, no other way unfortunately,' Simon calmly told her as the vehicle ground its way up the river with water above both headlights.

Climbing out of the river, the track was steep and dangerous but years of experience guided Simon, and the vehicle climbed its way up the sharp riverbank ever so slowly, eventually coming out on the other side; the occupants shaking their heads in disbelief at what they had just achieved.

'Simon, you've gotta do this again at some stage today and I can tell you, I am one happy person we won't be with you,' John whispered from a dry mouth.

'Not so bad the other way, at least we go down the really steep bit,' replied Simon casually as again the vehicle picked up speed.

The three travellers devoured the sandwiches and hot coffee prepared for the journey and took a short stop to attend to calls of nature. In this demanding and isolated part of the planet, people understood the realities of the situation and got on with it; no political correctness here.

The quick pit stop refreshed the occupants of the laden Land Cruiser and prepared them for the next section of the trip. Parts of the road allowed for higher speeds and once again, great numbers of buffalo and wild horses dotted the landscape. A heavy haze of smoke now began to appear as they entered a charred and burnt area of thousands of hectares; the fire had been so hot it had killed all the vegetation.

'What on earth has happened here Simon?' asked Betty sounding concerned.

'The Indigenous Ranger program; it's a program initiated by the former Gillard Government to employ local people,' replied Simon.

'*Really?* I thought you'd just passed legislation to tax carbon, and here we have *millions* of acres going up in smoke!' Betty exclaimed.

'Unfortunately it's happening in the Kimberley and here too. These hot fires destroy everything. I'm going to their camp at Mewal coming back, and will ask them not to burn my concession. I did it a bit earlier and it didn't cause so much damage as the burning wasn't so hot. I burn to attract game to the green grass but burn early so it's slow and not so destructive,' Simon advised.

'Why burn all this country now? Surely the Indigenous people don't have to burn to attract game to hunt nowadays?' asked John.

'No, it's just a scheme – one of the many – to employ local people and besides that, it's part of their culture to burn small areas on which to hunt,' answered Simon.

'What? Did they have helicopters and incendiaries and burn *so* much? I don't think so,' commented Betty.

Simon laughed, 'I guess not, and yes, it does seem strange that we introduce carbon tax then turn millions of acres into a holocaust spewing tons of carbon into the air! The worst part is that they'll begin dropping incendiaries again today but I trust not too close to the track we're taking.'

Glancing at his watch, Simon grasped that time was of the essence; he'd allowed for four hours but due to some tough and slow patches of the track, he would have to increase speed to reach the airstrip on the agreed time. All talk now ceased as they seemed to fly along, avoiding sizeable washouts and rocks, exposed by many wet seasons and no maintenance of the road. This was because no Aboriginal families lived outside the larger towns anymore, choosing to be near the services such as schools, health and supermarkets. Simon didn't blame them for not wanting to live in such isolated communities but he often wondered at those who progressed with such stupid ideas, wasting many millions of dollars. It was even amusing. Today, the Prime Minister was visiting Gove to look at Aboriginal housing. *Had he even looked out of the aircraft as it flew over hundreds of new homes, would he not have questioned why they lay abandoned?*

The appointed time had arrived and Simon knew he was still at least ten minutes from the main road that led to Katherine. The Land Cruiser pulled into the airstrip exactly twenty minutes late and the occupants gave a deep sigh; no sign of a plane on the runway. Simon imagined the worst. The inland mission was primarily used to transport sick or pregnant Aboriginal people to hospital and if they'd received a call, his clients would be regarded as secondary.

Alighting from the vehicle the strip was silent, no people or plane. Simon picked up the satellite phone and dialled his wife. After a brief talk, he returned to his deflated and tired clients.

'Not so bad after all, the plane will only be an hour late; had to transport a patient to Gove from here, so schedule back an hour,' Simon informed them.

They all breathed a sigh of relief and drank the last of the coffee.

'I have to visit one of the owners of my concession, would you like to come into Numbulwar with me?' Simon asked Betty and John.

'Love to! Never seen an Aboriginal town before, what an experience,' Betty replied full of enthusiasm.

Driving the short distance into town, Simon wanted to catch his friend and the elder of the group who owned his concession to pay the fee for the last hunt. Every buffalo and pig, plus any wild cattle, attracted a set figure for the Indigenous owners. Simon always liked to pay promptly, and doing so had maintained a good relationship over many years.

Calling in at the police station and grocery store, Betty and John followed Simon, hungrily noting every detail of daily life of the inhabitants. When Simon arrived at his old friend's home, Simon sat his visitors around the small fire that burned in the back yard and introduced them to George, the clan leader of the group who owned the land his concession operated on. The Americans noticed Simon pass the cheque to George and then discuss arrangements to pick him up later to go to the ranger program camp, and request that his concession *not* be fire bombed, thus driving all the game out.

With a new client arriving, Simon knew he would need to find buffalo and the animals would move long distances with the fires burning in his area. After the meeting and while sitting in the vehicle on their return trip to the airstrip, past sheds with road maintenance crews and the power station, John looked across at Simon and asked, 'Simon, why are all the workers white people? All the Indigenous people seem to be wandering around aimlessly doing nothing. The place is an absolute mess; surely they can pick up rubbish?'

'Would rather not start on that one,' Simon replied diplomatically.

'Incredible,' said John shaking his head in disbelief.

Back at the airport, the plane had just taxied to a stop and Simon noted Dee Fuller step out waving with his big smile, followed by a tall, good-looking woman. Greeting them, he helped unload their luggage onto the ground and with the help of Dee, loaded the Voss luggage into the plane.

Farewells over, Simon, Dee and Priscilla watched as the little aircraft taxied down the runway before hurtling down the strip and into the wide blue sky of the gulf.

Turning to Simon, Dee beamed and said, 'Ok Simon, here we go! I've warned Priscilla what we're in for!'

'I hope you don't mind Dee, I have to pick up George and call at Mewal and try and stop the ranger program guys from roasting my concession,' apologised Simon.

'No problem,' replied Dee replied. 'Our time is a bit open either way; we're in your capable hands.'

'Actually Dee, we may even camp the night at Mewal and leave early in the morning, do you mind?' Simon asked looking at the two of them.

'Whatever suits you Simon, we have no problems with

that,' said Dee looking at Priscilla who nodded and smiled.

Throwing the luggage into the back, they drove off back towards Numbulwar to pick up George. Simon was so pleased that his last client was an old friend. His companion seemed quiet and something about her intrigued him.

FIVE

Driving the short distance from the airstrip to the Indigenous town of Numbulwar, Simon pulled up outside one of the houses. Numbulwar was quite a substantial community and many residents owned houses on their tribal lands in the interior. The older members of the community had, from time to time, spent short periods on their traditional lands but the younger generation had no desire whatsoever to leave the town area. Actually, many had never even travelled outside the precincts of the town other than to travel by aircraft to Katherine or Gove; the bigger towns offering the availability and attraction of the scourge of all Indigenous communities – alcohol.

Simon left Dee and Priscilla in the vehicle and returned with an elderly Aboriginal couple. The man's beard was snowy white and the woman's hair was matted and silver. Simon introduced them to his clients as George and Mary and Priscilla was quite surprised to see that they had no food or camping gear other than a carton of cigarettes.

Although Mary was rather quiet, George was outgoing and a dialogue soon began on the way to the coastal camp, on land which was owned by George.

'Does all this land we are travelling through belong to you

George?' Priscilla asked. She was enjoying the rapport with the fascinating elderly Aboriginal.

'Me is the elder of my mob, and they go along with what I say,' George explained pointing out of the vehicle. 'This land here not ours; we start up coast further and it is about sixty kilometres long of coast.'

'Wow!' exclaimed Priscilla. 'How long since you have lived there?'

'Long time ago,' George replied. 'But we want to go there and live, no peace in town; young people banging on door all night, fighting, big problems.'

'Why don't you leave town and live out there then?' continued Priscilla.

'Me have no good car and government not build house out there yet on my country. Lots of others have houses way out but none for me on my country,' replied George.

During the journey, Priscilla gleaned that town life was becoming harder for the elders as the younger generation appears to have no respect or fear; even using standover tactics to take money off the older people. George told her that it was his and his wife's opinion that the only way was to return to tribal punishment of spearing miscreants in the leg with shovel-nosed spears. Managing to hide her shock, somehow Priscilla knew this would never eventuate.

The trip was long and the sun heated up the landscape although most of it was charred black, smoking and stark-looking. Simon told Dee and Priscilla that it was the result of helicopter incendiary dropping the previous day.

Dee and Simon chatted to each other while Priscilla sat in the back with the Aboriginal elders, admiring them for their quiet and unassuming natures. They had so many fascinating tales to tell and Priscilla was pleased that they were going to camp with them that evening. She looked forward to their invaluable information on the area and the Escarpment Country. Her inquisitive nature went into overdrive and she decided to ask George if he had met her father when he'd visited Numbulwar years before.

'I remember that fella,' George replied, his rheumy eyes smiling. 'He asked about them little fellas and I told him of being stalked by the little people years ago.'

Priscilla sank back in the seat, running her hands through her hair. Not only had her father been right, but she now sat next to the elder whom he had spoken to and verified his report. Priscilla noticed that Dee had overheard the conversation and gave her a quick glance. This, coupled with the information from the artist at Yirrkala, gave them high expectations of success. Priscilla knew not to pursue the matter further at this stage and settled into chatting about the land and its people.

Nothing had prepared Priscilla for the spectacle that appeared before them as they drove under a jungle-like cover of vegetation, crossed a crystal clear stream of water and then moved onto high sand dunes covered in grasses which flowed down to a beautiful white beach – the Gulf of Carpentaria. It was so beautiful it almost took Priscilla's breath away. She stepped out with the others, taking in the raw and wild beauty of Mewal.

Suddenly, two Aboriginal males came up the beach on quad bikes, stopping to see who the intruders were. On seeing Simon and George, they smiled.

'What you fellas doing?' George asked them.

'We doing survey of rubbish on the beach,' one replied.

'Why don't you pick it up?' Simon asked looking puzzled.

'No money to pick up rubbish, only do survey,' was the flat reply.

'Where is your camp?' continued Simon.

'Down over next rise, not far from your campsite George,' replied the other boy.

Simon then suggested they travel down the coast to a camp he had set up with a friend. He knew where the camp of the ranger program participants was and with George, he would request that they abstain from burning his concession. No one spoke as they slowly cruised down the coastal track. Priscilla appreciated why her two older companions would want to spend their last days in such a paradise, once inhabited by their past family members.

Getting back into the vehicle they drove off. Dee asked Simon, 'Why do they bother with the survey if they have no intention of picking up the rubbish?'

'Heaps of rubbish comes in off the trawlers; same each year with all the houses you'll see inland. Surveys are carried out each year to see what growth has grown around them and what fire hazard each settlement has. We have the surveys but nothing physical happens; the rubbish keeps piling up and the overgrowth envelopes new homes and it seems there is no money to do any work, only surveys,' answered Simon flatly.

Pulling up outside a cluster of tents and a helicopter parked nearby, Simon and George got out of the vehicle and approached some men who were standing around. Dee and Priscilla chatted to Mary as Simon and George had a discussion with the ranger program employees with regard to his concession.

Dee watched, as after their talk, they all shook hands. It appeared a compromise had been reached; Simon verified this when he got back to the vehicle and was noticeably happy with the outcome. A short drive later, the group pulled up under some magnificent shade trees where a gigantic tent with a table and chairs welcomed them. They unpacked their belongings into the tent while Priscilla looked on in awe. It was all so isolated and adventurous. *Why on earth had Dee impressed on her the challenges and difficulties they would face? This is wonderful,* she thought.

As it was lunchtime, Simon suggested that Dee and Priscilla might like to take a refreshing walk along the beach whilst he and George unpacked and prepared lunch. Mary was anxious to commence harvesting pandanus to dry as she still wove baskets and other handicrafts to supplement their income. Priscilla had already ordered a few of her beautiful baskets and paid in advance. She had never had close contact with full-blood tribal Aboriginals before and was so taken with George and Mary. She couldn't wait for their evening around the campfire to learn firsthand of their life and any information they had on the Stone People.

Leaving the camp hand in hand like two young lovers, Priscilla and Dee strolled over the coastal sand dunes and down onto the beach, stopping to take in the incredible beauty. The scene was indeed that of a picture book and terribly romantic. They stood in one of the most isolated places in the world. They decided to head south and so removed their heavy, hiking boots. The feel of the warm sand was too much and Dee suggested they take off their clothes and leave them with the boots. Priscilla smiled knowingly and accepted the invitation with a giggle. Stripping completely, the pair stood with their arms spread wide apart, totally free with the warm sun giving them a sensual sense of freedom.

'Dee, do you know what? I feel as though we are the *last people* on earth out here. I have never felt so totally free and uninhibited,' laughed Priscilla, twirling around with complete abandonment.

Wading into the aqua-coloured crystal clear water of the Gulf, they splashed each other playfully, staying in the shallows on Dee's instruction and watching out for crocodiles that inhabited this sector in large numbers.

Coming together in an embrace, Priscilla felt Dee's hardness against her and playfully dragged him onto the sand dunes. A tree had fallen off the bank and lying spread-eagled over the trunk, she drew Dee onto her hungry body. In one powerful thrust he entered her and their two bodies became one. Wildly engrossed and oblivious to the world, Dee rode her deeply as they groaned loudly in savage ecstasy.

Climaxing together, they clung on to each other to the very last, their bodies hot and sticky beneath the warm sun.

Staggering to his feet, Dee dragged Priscilla to her feet and pulled her into the refreshing water where they splashed and frolicked. The encounter had been brief but highly erotic and knew that it had served as a prelude to what would follow; the tryst only leaving them wanting more. As they strolled along the beach, neither spoke. Priscilla looked at Dee and for the first time in her life, clearly understood that against all odds, she had at last found her soul mate and was in love. For an hour they ambled, soaking up the atmosphere and each other's company; it was only when they reached an estuary that they decided to turn back.

At Priscilla's suggestion, they sat on a sand dune looking out to sea, holding hands but both aware that passion for intimacy was rising; fuelled by a fire that must be satisfied. Embracing, they kissed slowly and passionately. Priscilla placed her hand on his hardness, breathing in short, sharp breaths, expectant, wanting and ready to take her lover. Dee gently rolled Priscilla over onto all fours and drawing her buttocks towards him, spread her legs wide as she lay her head on her hands on the warm sand, giving small groans as Dee entered her from behind.

Gently and slowly they pleasured each other, pushing into each thrust, gradually building rhythm, completely lost in their ardour. Priscilla knew her climax was coming and looking back at Dee she groaned, 'Fuck me Dee and fuck me hard'.

Dee lustfully rose to the occasion and rode her like a

raging bull, the sound of her buttocks slapping against his thighs, sweat dripping off them as in one last mighty thrust, he ejaculated deep inside Priscilla who, when she felt the stickiness deep inside her, groaned in rapture as she shuddered in an exquisite orgasm. Dee rolled over and lay beside her, the two of them panting in the afterglow.

Priscilla had only experienced such total sexual satisfaction a few times in her life but this time she felt an inner glow that was foreign to her previous liaisons. She was now convinced that in Dee she had found her life partner and was sure the feeling was mutual. Having refreshed themselves in the water and collected their clothes, they lazily made their way back to camp. The sun was low in the sky and the aroma of fresh fish filled the air.

Looking up at the approaching couple, Simon called out, 'I was about to send out a search party but Mary told us you were safe and on your way back. George speared some fish and they're nearly ready.'

Priscilla looked at Mary who gave her a sheepish grin. It then struck Priscilla that Mary, in her pandanus gathering, had possibly seen their lovemaking, as a giant stand of pandanus grew on the rise overlooking the beach.

The fish dinner was enjoyed by everyone and Priscilla and Dee found their hosts to be so friendly and warm. Not only had she met her soul mate but meeting George and Mary had changed her attitude to Indigenous Australians. She found them astute, kind, caring and open towards strangers and they chatted long into the night. They learned so much about the area with its various tribes and the much-feared Stone People of the Escarpment Country. Priscilla had no idea that a Japanese submarine lay offshore, sunk by Australian Air Force planes based in Darwin during World War II. George's family had been on the beach and witnessed the battle; a cairn existed on the rise above, pointing to the war grave.

Priscilla's affinity with George and Mary grew as she learned more about them. The opinion of the general public was biased in that not *all* Aborigines depended on the authorities as a "cop out" for an easy life because by doing so, they were basically relinquishing any control or say that they have in their own lives.

The Aboriginal industry in Australia is a multi-billion dollar entity with thousands of faceless autocrats impacting on every aspect of their lives, feasting off taxpayer dollars and labeling anyone who questions it, a racist.

During the evening tête-à-tête, Priscilla noted that George often quoted "White Aboriginals" who appeared to have more influence and control of the destiny of the Aboriginal people than the full-blooded ones themselves. She sensed a growing divide amongst the groups.

It was nearly midnight before Simon suggested they turn in; Priscilla and Dee knew he was right, as a big day lay ahead.

Shouting goodnights, Priscilla snuggled up to Dee and ruminated over the day's events. Tomorrow's task brought a frown to her lovely face as she concerned herself with the possible effect her findings could have on her two special friends. She was worried. Maybe keeping the status quo was a better option. As she drifted off to sleep, she did wonder about the impact her uncovering might have; *should* they be successful.

SIX

Priscilla woke with a start. Looking at her watch it was seven am and she knew that Simon wanted to start early, as he had to take George and Mary back to Numbulwar before heading to his camp well inland. Shaking Dee she started to dress. The delicious aroma of freshly brewed coffee wafted invitingly into her tent and she could hear Simon talking to George. *Oh great, breakfast!* Sweeping the tent opening aside, Priscilla glanced back at Dee who was struggling to get into his clothes, disorientated at being so abruptly disturbed from a deep sleep. The two men smiled at Priscilla as Simon passed her a cup of steaming coffee.

'Did ya have a good night's sleep?' asked George sincerely.

'Fine thanks George. What a wonderful country you have here George. I thank you for sharing it with us,' replied Priscilla wrapping her hands around the mug.

'No worries, you welcome anytime,' George replied as he saw Dee coming out of the tent, shading his eyes from the bright sunlight.

The usual morning banter continued. It would take several hours to reach base camp and Priscilla was conscious that Simon was anxious to get on the road, but her eggs and bacon were scrumptious! Priscilla noticed bundles of pandanus neatly tied in the back of the Land Cruiser. The overnight luggage had somehow been fitted onto an already overloaded vehicle.

On the way into Numbulwar, Priscilla chatted with George and Mary and wondered why Australia seemed to be two distinct nations, each with its own flag, boundaries and in some cases, rules. On the way into the settlement of Numbulwar, they passed an old Holden dragging a colossal turtle on its back into town. The hapless animal was still alive.

'They can still legally hunt turtle and dugong,' Simon informed them.

'What are they doing with it?' Priscilla asked worryingly.

'Take him back to town and leave him on back to keep fresh until cook em up,' said George dispassionately.

Priscilla never pursued the fate of the turtle any further but wondered why traditional hunting still occurred when dugongs and indeed turtles, were becoming endangered. She noticed that the aluminium dinghy and steel spears were hardly traditional hunting! Why the need when there are well stocked supermarkets and takeaways in all the towns. *If we are*, she thought, *to become one society, then surely the same rules should apply to all people, regardless of race.*

Dropping off George and Mary at their home in Numbulwar, they said their goodbyes, promising to catch up again after the safari. Priscilla knew instinctively that old George was no fool and before they left, he turned to her and said softly but firmly, 'You be careful, that bad country, big problems there.'

Priscilla frowned. As they drove off into the interior, she felt uneasy at the old man's frown and genuine unease; however, taking in the stunning scenery, she felt committed. *There was no turning back now*, she thought resolutely.

Soon the rough bush track became a test of their guide's driving skills. Years traversing this country had made Simon an expert. They crossed a few small creeks before the smell of smoke made its way through the vehicle windows. Simon cursed. He knew that the helicopter was dropping incendiaries close by, as dozens of cane toads had crowded onto the track. The smell of acrid smoke filled the vehicle.

'I'm close to Harris Creek. I'll try and get us there so we can shelter until this fire passes,' Simon yelled above the roar of the fire, now approaching fast.

Dee gave Priscilla a worried look as the vehicle bumped and groaned its way around burning trees. With the windows wound up, the interior of the vehicle was becoming uncomfortable; the smell of smoke and heat was claustrophobic but the occupants remained silent as sweat streamed down their faces. Priscilla pictured the old Aboriginal George and his message. *Had he had an omen of what was to come?* Priscilla never imagined a fire could be so fast in coming. Suddenly, out of the thick smoke, the vehicle seemed to hang in mid-air, then it plunged straight down into a fast-flowing river that luckily only came up to the doors. Frantically throwing open the doors, all three jumped out into the cool water and stood coughing and spluttering as they desperately gasped for air. Priscilla and Dee heard Simon cursing at the stupidity of those who knew they would be travelling there today, for being so careless and causing the inferno that nearly cost them their lives.

'Stupid fucking government and their stupid fucking Indigenous programs! What the *fuck* are they gaining from burning country out here for fuck's sake!' he puffed.

Priscilla stood shaking in the cool flowing water. Dee wiped her streaming eyes with a wet cloth and they held each other close.

'Told you it can get rough out here,' he croaked.

'Traditional burns my fucking arse! With helicopters and incendiaries burning thousands of acres each day. *Fuck off!*' Simon shouted at no one.

Gaining their composure, they scrambled back into the vehicle which luckily was still running in the metre-high water. Simon skillfully drove down the river until an opening appeared on the opposite bank. Tilting the vehicle into the opening, they came out the other side and looked back at what they had escaped; the whole bank opposite was one sheet of flame. A cold chill ran down their spines as they had now entered Simon's concession which "they" had promised *not* to burn for another month.

For some time the track travelled across open country with several tracks veering off from the main one. Simon informed them that there were houses there but that they were abandoned or had never been lived in. At midday, they came to a village which had several new homes as well as some older ones but they were all empty. Mango trees grew amongst the homes, and a generator still sat in one of the sheds which was now being used as shelter by wild buffalo. In the centre sat a telephone box. Then, to Priscilla and Dee's amazement, Simon told them he had to make a couple of phone calls! Apparently, it was still maintained by Telstra in case the Indigenous owners decided one day to return.

While Simon made his calls, Priscilla and Dee walked around the village and saw that it even had a playground. Some of the homes had locks but most didn't, yet they all seemed in relatively good order. They noticed a copse of Cypress Pine used, Dee informed Priscilla, by Simon as wood for his camp fire. It gave off a wonderful aroma when burning.

'Better aroma I hope than the last fire,' laughed Priscilla. With the ordeal over, her spirits rose again but facing death changes one's perspective and Priscilla felt so much closer to Dee; the scare had actually brought them closer than ever.

Dee and Priscilla enjoyed a cold drink and snack while Simon finished his calls; he seemed more settled on his return. 'My daughter won a school race!' he proudly boasted. 'I'll be glad to get back to family life for a while,' he quipped.

'Sorry Simon to extend your time out here but I now feel we must be honest with you,' announced Priscilla.

'I'm aware of your plans, just by your conversations with George and you may not be aware but when I heard your late father's name, I knew you were on a quest,' laughed Simon.

'I'll pay you well. Do you think any of the Stone People still exist?' asked Priscilla eagerly.

'I would say definitely. Don't forget, George and his companion had an encounter only fifteen years ago, and although I've never told anyone, three years ago I had an American client on the fringe up there and we came across a small fire which was only days old; it nearly cost us our life,' said Simon.

The hairs stood up on Priscilla's head; she felt sure, that with a bit of luck, she really might be able to prove her father's theory that the Stone People were of different origins to the coastal tribes.

Hours later, after crossing wetlands and the fast, flowing Walker River, they eventually arrived at Simon's safari camp. Throughout her whole career, Priscilla had never been in a more isolated spot before; it was almost unearthly to know one was so far from civilisation. Simon lit a fire and in no time, they all enjoyed a refreshing shower, followed by a couple of bottles of wine and shaved buffalo meat. They sat under the stars, listening to crocodiles barking in the river below and the sad, wailing cry of a buffalo calf being dragged down by a dingo pack.

Priscilla was in awe of the remoteness and wildness she now found herself in and wondered if it *were* possible for a number of Stone People to still be surviving, west of their location, in the inhospitable Escarpment Country, only fifty kilometres away.

Simon suggested that they all lie in the following morning

because if, as he had expected, they wanted an expedition into the Escarpment Country, it would take a day to prepare; supplies had to be packed including basic first-aid equipment. Dee and Simon each had satellite phones and wanted to ensure the batteries were fully charged. A successful preparation could mean the difference between success and disaster. Even if help was called for, the time factor in finding them could possibly be days.

As they undressed and snuggled into each other's arms; sex was the last thing on their minds. A sense of trepidation embraced them but they gained strength from the close bond they now shared. In the past, Dee had hunted in a thirty-kilometre radius of the camp yet now, the task ahead seemed monumental. They talked for some time before fatigue got the better of them and they drifted into a troubled sleep.

SEVEN

The steady drum of the generator was the first sound Priscilla heard when she woke; shards of sunlight crept through the tent opening. During the night, Dee had placed a leg over her and now she gently lifted it off. Priscilla smiled as she looked at her dozing companion, sure he would sleep through a cyclone.

Dressing quietly, Priscilla made the walk to the toilet which was set up some distance away. Sitting on the seat, she surveyed the scene before her over the structure that afforded the basics of modesty, yet provided a good view of the camp. A dingo slinked slowly through the camp, ready to scavenge any morsels left by the occupiers. Simon was sitting by a fire outside the main lodge drinking his morning coffee and listening to ABC World News on his shortwave radio.

Like the calm before the storm, she thought, *such a peaceful and isolated place in a savage land.* She wondered about the people who had walked this land before white man came, and how they were able to wage war with each other with their deadly shovel-nosed spears over some incident, yet which would soon be forgotten and done with.

It is possible that Syd Kyle-Little had been correct in his warnings about the importance of keeping the Aboriginals in their homeland. They were hunter-gatherers and not meant to drift into "white" society but the alleged experts disregarded this. It was and still is their destruction, Priscilla sadly thought, but then a clash of two such different societies would invariably prove to be disastrous. If the British had not claimed Australia as its own, it would be fanciful to claim that no other nation would not have done the same, and that the consequences for the Aboriginals could possibly have been far worse.

Patricia noticed Dee suddenly appear outside their tent and shading his eyes from the sun, scanned around, no doubt looking for her. A smile came over her face as she shuffled to the door and flashed him! Dee threw his head back laughing and gave her the finger. Priscilla was so in love and fortunately they shared the same good sense of humour – at their age and stage of life, all inhibitions long gone.

After a leisurely breakfast, Dee accompanied Simon to a shed which was situated across a stream and adjacent to the main camp, to assist with packing enough equipment for at least a week or more. They'd decided to rough it and use single person tents and sleeping bags which each individual would carry into the Escarpment Country as well as enough food.

From information passed on by Dee and Simon, Priscilla gleaned that a small settlement existed only a short stroll away on the bank of a wide billabong. She decided to explore the area. The sun was well up and as she strolled along a well-defined track, Priscilla felt relaxed and happier than she had been in a long time. Dee was her first serious relationship and she believed strongly that at this juncture of her life, she had found the right man. Recalling previous relationships, some that she would rather forget, Dee was in fact, the first man to truly fulfill her sexual needs. Others had disappointed her or had just behaved distastefully.

Lost in thought, she suddenly froze, aware that within metres of her, a buffalo cow and calf stood peacefully under the shade of a tree. They stared straight at her. Unsure what to do, Priscilla held her breath and remained motionless for what felt like forever, before the two animals bolted into the bush. Breathing heavily, she cursed her daydreaming and apathy, knowing full well that the meeting could have been life-threatening. Buffalo, in many circumstances when frightened, can charge and Priscilla knew that several people had been killed previously by animals reacting to fear.

When Priscilla eventually reached the settlement, she sat on the verandah of one of the houses. She was still trembling. As she looked around at the scene before her; two near-new homes with outside shower blocks and two loos for each dwelling sat in a clearing overlooking a lagoon. Both homes had solar systems on the roofs and lockable gates surrounded the porches. *How on earth had all this material been delivered to such an isolated area?* wondered Priscilla. Regaining her composure, she decided not to let Simon or Dee know of her stupidity and carelessness. She strolled over to the lagoon and was reminded again of the dangers that exist in the wilderness, as a crocodile glided past boldly and unafraid of her presence.

It was late afternoon when she reached the main camp; her return trip had been taken extremely cautiously. Simon and Dee were sitting at the table overlooking the Walker River, calmly drinking coffee and chatting, while a monster salty cruised gracefully up the river below. Making herself a coffee, she joined them and listened to their stories of past hunts and times shared. Priscilla discerned that the two men had formed a close alliance over the years and held each other in high regard.

The sun set slowly over the Escarpment Country as they wined and dined before turning in for an early night; another big day ahead. Dee caught Priscilla by the hand as they neared their tent and stopped to give her a long, hard kiss. Priscilla glowed with happiness as the tent flap opened and they stepped inside. She knew what was to come, and eagerly dropped her clothes on the floor and slid into bed.

A barking crocodile woke up Priscilla. She was comfy and did not want to leave her bed. Days of discomfort and danger lay ahead and they would be exploring one of the most remote regions of Australia; an area visited by no more than a few white people since the settlement of this great land.

Dressing hastily, she knew that Simon was already up and waiting for her and Dee to make an appearance. Dee dressed silently. They were equally a little more than hesitant at the prospect of spending the following week in such unforgiving country. If the truth be known, Priscilla had begun to go off the whole idea but knew that she was responsible and could not renege at this stage. She pulled herself together and put on a happy, positive face.

Their hearty breakfast of bacon and eggs was eaten in silence. Simon had painstakingly packed the vehicle with adequate supplies. He had to admit to being a little anxious, due to his previous two forays into the Escarpment Country, as they had both ended badly. This time, he convinced himself that he had taken adequate precautions so as not to have a repeat of his last experiences. The sun had just reached its full height when they drove out of the safari camp ground and headed west with the sun at their backs. Priscilla lapped up the ever-changing landscape of thick, dry bush suddenly clearing to open plains, with herds of buffalo and occasional wild pigs and cattle, scurrying at the sound of the vehicle intruding into their domain. After several hours, and with her heartbeat rapidly increasing, Priscilla noticed the towering Escarpment Country looming closer than ever as they crossed rivers and climbed over land where vegetation tapered off dramatically. Dee pointed out to her how the animal life had gradually dwindled too, as they left the more fertile plains behind them.

They came to an abrupt halt at three pm. The track had ended and before them lay a sharp incline of rocks and sandy country; devoid of vegetation. Much to the relief of Priscilla and Dee, Simon suggested they call it a day and unpack and prepare their packs for the next morning. They'd been tossed around mercilessly in the truck as the track had become more rough and demanding. Two deserted houses were most welcome as their shelter.

Simon cooked up a simple meal of dried vegetables and pasta before sipping on sweet Billy tea. By now, the last of the sun's rays had eerily disappeared as they spread their sleeping bags on the porch of one of the houses. Sleep did not come easily to any of them. Apprehension at what was facing them loomed at the forefront of their minds.

After a night of tossing and turning, Priscilla ached all over as she awoke with a start. Glancing over at Dee, she saw that he was still asleep but that Simon was missing. Fully dressed, she struggled up out of her sleeping bag, her bones stiff and sore, she peered into the morning light lazily waiting for the hazy images before her to manifest. Simon was standing by the vehicle staring into the distance. Walking up to him she asked, 'What can you see Simon?'

'Nothing really. Just had a feeling something was about,' he replied, his eyes scanning.

Priscilla noticed that Simon's rifle was slung over his shoulder and dismissed it as a wild animal circling the camp; something she knew buffalo and dingoes often do, even at the main camp.

'Let's have some breakfast and get going. It can get *really* hot out here in the middle of the day,' warned Simon.

Dee had heard their talk and was already up on their return with the billycan on the fire and some cereal in three bowls; a quick breakfast today.

With breakfast over, and their heavy backpacks strapped on, Dee and Priscilla formed a line behind Simon. They headed over the rise towards the sheer wall of the escarpment, some ten kilometres away. It was heavy going right from the start and Simon stopped several times in order for Priscilla and Dee to catch up; the heat began to rise and sweat trickled down their anxious faces.

'Spread the water out as much as possible,' Simon advised them. 'I'm sure we can top up at some of the springs ahead but just in case, conserve as much as you can'.

'I'm sure it'll be a bit cooler in the escarpment,' Dee replied encouragingly.

'Unfortunately, in the narrow gorges it's stifling and I may wait until evening to enter when it's cooler,' said Simon panting.

Three hours later they came face to face with a sheer wall; absolutely impossible to scale. Sitting down in the shade, Simon suggested they have a short break and then head north to an opening he knew into the interior of the Escarpment Country. Simon confessed to never having gone that far before and wasn't sure how far they might have to travel, once through the opening.

Priscilla staggered to her feet first. 'Come on you lot, no use sitting here,' she said dryly and promptly strode south towards the area Simon had pointed out.

After another gruelling hour, they stood before an enormous split in the solid rock; a narrow entrance with sheer walls on either side opened before them. No one spoke as Simon entered the passage; Dee and Priscilla recalling his earlier warning as the hot, dry air hit them. Priscilla glanced up and saw a thin streak of daylight above. So narrow was the track that it soon became gloomy with just enough room to pass through, but where passage became impossible, they had to struggle over boulders and rubbish that had fallen from above. The only sound was that of their heavy breathing. Priscilla stopped for several drinks as her throat felt constantly dry and the back of her legs began to cramp.

They were covered in sweat and the air was fetid. There was no escaping the pungent smell and after absolute ages, Simon finally stopped in a small cavity and all three slumped to the ground.

'Do you want to go on?' asked Simon looking at Priscilla.

'Simon,' she gasped, 'I *do* have regrets and feel that I was a tad hasty in my quest but I *am* committed and would never forgive myself if I quit.'

'Well said my love,' Dee butted in.

'Ok, just thought I'd ask now because things'll get worse. This is inhospitable country; I'd guess we're the first to ever enter here, apart from the original Stone People,' smiled Simon mischievously.

'Right,' Simon encouraged them, 'it'll get freezing in here tonight. I'm sure we can break out into some open area and get a fire going.'

Gamely they battled on. The light began to disappear as the sun began its descent. It was almost pitch black when Simon pointed to an opening and with renewed strength, they picked up pace. Ploughing ahead, they kicked aside small flakes of stone off the cramped track as they filed along.

Priscilla became despondent. *Was there really an opening? How much farther?* With fierce determination she soldiered on, deep in thought as to *why* she really had to finish her adventure not only out of respect for her late father but her own peace of mind. Eventually, and in the light from Simon's torch, they broke into an opening. Unable to see anything apart from what the small light the torch produced, they gathered sticks from the little shrubs that surrounded them and fell into a heap by the fire as soon as it sprung into life. It seemed they had entered an enormous amphitheatre. Dee and Priscilla readily agreed with Simon's suggestion to rest that night and "check out" the surroundings come morning. Too tired to even take off their clothes; they downed some health bars, and scooping a small indent in the soft sand, climbed into their sleeping bags. Within minutes, the two were sound asleep.

Simon remained by the fire for some time. He looked over at his two travelling companions, asleep in the firelight. A gentle smile came over his face; a veteran of many nights under the stars with clients from all over the world, he was pleased that they shared some grit and determination. He knew they would need to rely on it before this trip was over. Gathering up some more sticks, he stacked the pile by the fire and scooping a bed into the sand, laid his sleeping bag out. Before climbing inside and zipping it up, he placed his rifle next to him, not quite sure why he felt the need to. Just as he was about to lie down, a slight, subtle breeze came up and he sat bolt upright. The unmistakable smell of a human wafted in the slight swirl of air; it seemed close and he was sure it did not come from the direction of his companions on the other side of the fire.

Slowly easing out of his sleeping bag, he dragged it over to the wall close by and sitting in the darkness, tried to survey the scene before him. Unfortunately it was a really dark night and apart from the flickering light of the small fire, he was unable to see anything. Cautiously, he opened his rucksack and feeling for his phone, turned it on; cursing its display of "no signal". Not wanting to alarm his exhausted clients, Simon sat silently clutching his rifle and slipped the safety catch off. Over the years he'd heard stories of the "little people" and like most sceptics, was sure they no longer existed, but at this very moment he was certainly doubtful. Out there in the dark he knew eyes were watching them; waiting. Unsure of what their intentions could be towards intruders, Simon decided to keep watch all night.

Simon kept the fire burning at all times. Despite the lateness, he was fully alert; decades of hunting had kept his senses and instinct sharp. He knew that someone was out there; furthermore, he knew it could only be the feared Stone People – the pygmies of the escarpment area – the very people the woman who slept soundly before him had come to discover. Simon was fully aware that sheer luck had brought them to this area of the Escarpment Country; hundreds of kilometres long, wild, and unfathomed.

To keep himself from dozing off, Simon would stand and stretch and then wash his face in cold water, remembering how precious the resource was. He was tempted to wake up Dee to take over, as he thought him quite capable but then Priscilla would no doubt wake up and three wide awake people would not help the situation; far better to keep a lid on things and remain quiet. He was sure nothing would happen now in the dark. Surely it would have happened before now. In all his life, Simon was never so happy to see the first signs of daylight start to appear; streaks of light began to light up the amphitheatre in a spectacular way. Dee and Priscilla stirred and sat up rubbing their eyes and looking around at the area they had stumbled into last night.

They peeled off their sleeping bags and stumbled towards the fire rubbing their hands; it was rather chilly.

Simon approached them and in hushed words told of his long night. Dee and Priscilla nervously glanced around their camp area, their imaginations running riot.

'Simon, I can smell that smell too!' Priscilla exclaimed

'I can too; it's coming from close by!' cried Dee.

About fifty metres from their camp, Simon saw a cave, and covering his mouth for the others to keep quiet, picked up his rifle and torch and walked to the entrance. Priscilla and Dee followed Simon into the cave. It was long, and at the back of it, some hundred metres away, ran an underground stream. It ran slowly and into the adjoining wall. As they followed the stream, they were horrified to discover a small female lying on the sand, barely breathing. On examination, she had a horrific wound to her right leg which was covered in puss and the smell was sickening. Carefully, they carried the frail, delicate body out into the sunlight and gently placed her by the fire.

Priscilla immediately began to make her comfortable as Simon broke open the first-aid kit. Her wound was cleaned and swabbed with antiseptic cream before bandaging it securely. Simon broke a vial of antibiotics and drawing a needle, injected the fragile figure. Although Royal Flying Doctor first-aid kits required a doctor's permission to administer such treatment, under the circumstances, they unanimously agreed it was vital.

Priscilla had a spare blanket and after making the girl comfortable, gave her a cup of sweet tea which she swallowed slowly. Priscilla was saddened by her wide, sad eyes that gazed at her, seemingly without recognition. She took photos of her patient and gently drew a blood sample from her. During the day they fed her mashed food and gradually she responded to their care.

Simon investigated the area while Dee and Priscilla stayed with the young woman. When he returned, he told them that a well-worn exit ran south of their position, trafficked by animals and humans. Above their position, a long shelf ran nearly the entire length of the gap in the escarpment.

Questions plagued them. *What had happened to her* and *Why had she been left to die?* Simon went back to the cave for some water and it was markedly obvious that it had been used before by other humans. Remnants of fires were scattered throughout the cave as well as small animal bones. He then discovered several tracks that made their way up to the ridge above them and at least four other caves were visible.

During lunch, they discussed the best plan of action. Their special patient was their priority and accepted that it would take a few days for her to recover. They agreed most passionately too, that to take her away from her people and into white society or that of her enemies was not a good idea.

As they ate in silence, Priscilla watched Simon as he picked up his rifle and took careful aim at the ridge above. Priscilla swung with her camera and saw two small figures far above watching them. Expertly and with speed, she managed to take three shots with her telephoto lens, as she had only taken some photos of the area earlier that day. Priscilla jumped as she heard the rifle go off, reverberating around the amphitheatre. Glancing up at the ridge, the figures had disappeared and a rock wallaby fell below onto the ground with a thud.

'Just letting them know that we are *not* easy pickings,' said Simon. 'Around here we are definitely sitting ducks but all being well, that'll deter them.'

'Bloody fine shot Simon!' exclaimed Dee in awe.

'Frightened the hell out of me,' blurted Priscilla. 'I'm sure it will have the same effect on the little fellas.'

'These guys are warlike; this may help us,' said Simon.

For two days they attended to the patient, cleaning and bandaging her wounds. On the second day, with Priscilla's help, she managed to use the toilet and Priscilla knew that she was becoming attached to the young girl. Attending to her every need, she was rewarded with a soft smile but the young girl did not utter a word or sound.

EIGHT

On day four, Priscilla woke to find Simon and Dee fast asleep; they were supposed to have been keeping guard. Looking over to check on her patient, Priscilla's heart skipped a beat; she was gone!

Priscilla was heartbroken. She had become a mother figure to her but Simon, in his infinite wisdom told her that it was probably far better this way; at least she was with her own people. To introduce her to their world would have destroyed her.

Priscilla knew he was right. This place was like another planet and there was no way she would have adapted to the outside world. Even so, a sombre mood embraced them as they packed to leave; their trip so far exceeding their every expectation.

Priscilla looked at Simon and said solemnly, 'Simon, we've come so far and *never* in my wildest dreams did I think we'd achieve such success. Before we leave this place, may I have an extra day to investigate the caves above? We have enough food for another three days and it would be impossible to try and find this place again.' With bated breath she waited for his reply; her heart in her mouth.

To her absolute relief, Simon replied, 'Absolutely right

Priscilla! I'm interested in doing the same and hope it'll answer a few questions. I don't think the little people come here much as there is very little evidence of them in the area.'

Stacking their equipment and packs by the entrance to the cave and only carrying water, they began the ascent on one of the small tracks leading to the shelf which was only thirty metres above them. The shelf then appeared to widen and wind its way to the top of the escarpment. They found it laborious as it was near impossible to gain solid footing; loose gravel and stone crumbled and fell away with each laboured step. What initially had seemed an easy climb, took them over one hour as they constantly had to help each other.

When they finally reached the shelf, it was narrow at first and in one place, had fallen away leaving a precarious path held together only by tree roots. Gingerly, Simon went ahead and held out a strong arm so the others might have some safety net as they picked their way over the track. Once on the other side, it was apparent that as they had expected, human traffic had been using it and only recently. Dee even found two new sets of footprints which had obviously been left by the two who had been observing them far below.

The first cave they came across was not very big, and a few handprints could be discerned on the dry interior surface. Small fires had been lit inside and were recent. Priscilla carefully photographed everything, trying not to disturb anything but to leave it as they had found it. Simon had gone on ahead and returned excitedly, 'Come quick, you will *not* believe what's in the next cave – it's so big!'

Dee and Priscilla followed Simon to the next cave and on entering it, stood speechless. The cave *was* huge, with a high ceiling although the entrance was narrow. In the dim light it took a while for their eyes to adjust and then they stood silently, taking in what lay before them.

Several shelf-like stone burial caverns had been carved into the walls; each one stacked neatly with hundreds of bones. They had stumbled across a burial ground. Had the girl had been left to die and could the two "observers" have possibly returned to place her with her ancestors, thinking she would be dead?

Priscilla continued to take many photos; humbled by the discovery of an ancient burial ground of the little people. No one spoke.

'I actually feel uncomfortable that we've trespassed on the site of their ancestors,' Priscilla said to the others as she documented on camera their finding. They knew that this area was only used for burial and was taboo to the little people other than delivering their ancestors to their final resting place.

Small skulls had been lined up neatly in rows and the air hung heavy with a putrid aroma. For two hours they scrutinised the caves; the temperature within being ideal to preserve the bones. Priscilla surmised that some of the earlier burials could have been performed thousands of years earlier, with the numbers most likely being much bigger at that time. The lack of evidence of any recent burials indicated that burial numbers must now be critically low.

It was actually Simon who had to suggest they move on if they wanted to explore the two other caves higher up; begrudgingly, Priscilla agreed. What they had encountered in this cave alone was a piece of unknown history that could change the way most Australians think.

A search of the other caves found them relatively small although each contained the imprint of small hands; the only art or signs left by the inhabitants. They all showed signs of human use over the centuries but little present-day use.

Making their way down the track back to camp, they were incredibly thrilled to know that they would have been the only "modern" humans to walk into the cave and Priscilla was especially cognisant that to disclose the find would lead to the destruction of the last of the little people.

Simon headed the walk back, cautiously making his way over the parts that were most dangerous. Priscilla stepped forward to catch hold of his arm which he had extended towards her but she slipped before getting a secure hold. Her foot became entangled in a tree root and Simon and Dee watched in horror as she fell forward, saved by her entangled foot from falling to her death below. A sickening crack filled the area as her ankle snapped under the strain; Priscilla felt the pain shoot up her leg and her last vision was the open space beneath her as she passed out.

With super human effort, the men dragged Priscilla back up onto a safe part of the ledge. They sat either side of her while they caught their breath, sweating profusely.

'Stay with her Dee. I'll go below and get our swags and

gear; it may take a while. We can't return the way we came as it's single file only and tough. I think we can get her to the top and I'll phone up and get a helicopter to pick us up. Give me the water containers that are empty and I'll fill them up. I'm sure the satellite phones will work on top.'

Dee nodded, still in shock at their changed circumstances. They were in big trouble now; even to get Priscilla to the top was going to be hard going.

Simon disappeared down the track as Dee splashed water over Priscilla's face. She looked almost angelic, white as a ghost and breathing with shallow gasps. Slowly, after what, Priscilla opened her eyes and immediately began to sob uncontrollably.

'Oh Dee, I'm so sorry! This is all *my* fault… if it hadn't been for me, Simon would be home with his family and you my darling would be back in America.'

Dee smiled. 'Priscilla my love, we're all adults here with our own minds. I would *never* have missed this and we might not have got together. I may as well tell you now, but when we got back, I was going to propose but now seems as good a time as any.'

Priscilla stopped crying and looked earnestly at Dee, 'Not bullshitting me *again* lover, are you?'

'Never more serious in my life. Time I settled down; stuff this adventure crap! If we get out of this one, a more sedate life chasing you around the bedroom is called for!' he grinned cheekily. Priscilla smiled weakly.

'Dee, we *will* make it! Simon knows what he's doing but

how are we going to explain how we came to be here when the rescue helicopter comes?' Priscilla replied.

'Let's cross each hurdle as we come to it my love; I am, as you say, a good bullshitter,' laughed Dee.

After what seemed like hours and with darkness approaching, Simon returned out of breath and minus any camp gear.

'It's all gone!' he exclaimed breathlessly. 'Satellite phones, rifle, the lot … all I was able to do was fill the canteens with water.'

Priscilla was in deep pain and all three felt vulnerable and were aware of the absolute danger they now faced.

Simon spoke first. 'Okay, the best we can do is to make it to the top; if we can find some water, I'll leave you there and go for help. On my own I can travel fast but firstly we must get to the top. I suggest, as it will be dark soon, we start *now* and travel as far as we can.'

'Leave me here,' Priscilla told them. 'I *cannot* endanger your lives further.'

Dee promptly replied, 'We *both* get out or *both* stay here old girl. I just proposed, so leaving you here isn't an option.'

Locking arms, Dee and Simon made a chair for Priscilla. Luckily they were pretty fit and Priscilla's slight frame helped but even so, the climb was arduous. One thing was in their favour and that was a full moon. Its light guided them up the steep incline to the top of the escarpment.

Despite the temperature dropping, sweat rose from the two men as finally they came out onto a rim above the amphitheatre. Even in the moonlight they were unable to see all the way to the bottom. The area now seemed so small and so well hidden even from the air; it could have been their tomb.

Utterly exhausted and with Priscilla drifting in and out of consciousness, they decided to sleep in a small incline amongst the rocks and then in daylight, survey the area and make plans for their next move. Simon knew that if he didn't get the couple rescued in the next two days, the trip could end fatally.

Making themselves as comfortable as possible they tried to sleep. Priscilla was in great pain but was kept warm by Dee who pulled her as close to him as possible; the night became colder and a sense of desperation came over them.

Simon did not sleep well that night. He knew, from his lifetime of experience in this area, exactly what would be needed to make it out and back to the vehicle and then to drive to the settlement on the walker and call for help. He knew that they were several kilometres from the escarpment drop-off onto the plains below with a good day back to the phone. What truly troubled him was their supply of water; his clients would only last two days at the most. He frowned with deep concern; it seemed almost impossible.

NINE

Unable to sleep and worried about Priscilla who groaned all through the night, Simon gently woke Dee at four am.

'Dee, I'm going now. Shh, we have no chance unless I leave now. You have two containers of water and I'll take the half empty flask; with luck, I can reach the vehicle site by nightfall tonight, if I travel all night I can make it to the deserted camp and the phone booth by tomorrow morning. Somehow, you *have* to hold on,' informed Simon gravely.

The two men stood up and shook hands then Simon marched off into the black, heading east towards the first light of day which was barely visible on the horizon.

Dee again lay down next to Priscilla trying to keep her warm until the sun, in its full force, would result in the opposite problem here on top of the escarpment; he knew it would be boiling hot by midday.

****

Simon kept up a steady pace, dodging around rocky outcrops, mindful of the task that lay ahead and his responsibility for the survival of those he had left behind. Several times he had to detour around deep chasms in the ancient landscape. The other worry for Simon was how exposed and defenceless they were if the little people decided to attack. It was common knowledge, from past reports, of the fear the coastal tribes held for the little people in the Debil Debil country; another worry.

Simon's job became easier when the first rays of daylight spread slowly over the land; a land he had never journeyed before in his life and doubted if any others, if at all, had walked the same ground. The terrain was not flat as he had initially envisaged; massive stone outcrops shot into the sky and there were deep gorges, blasted over centuries by wet seasons and high winds. Several times he stopped to survey the landscape and knew by the sun that he was heading east in the right direction. Climbing over a ridge, Simon at last saw the plains below but peering into the haze he cursed, as in the distance he saw smoke rising and realised that the area of his camp was on fire.

Maintaining a fast pace, Simon kept his drinking to a minimum, sipping water only when he truly had to. The sun began to beat mercilessly down on him and, even the rocks he passed radiated intense heat. Simon's experience led him to believe that water in this area had long since dried up and what he had would have to last the distance, possibly a third of what he would require but he knew he had to leave the supply they had with Dee. Simon was determined not to stop. He had been called pigheaded and stubborn but for now, his drive to get off the escarpment and get help kept him moving forward.

It was mid-afternoon when with immense relief; he saw the edge of the escarpment. Quickening his pace, his jaw dropped when he got to the edge. He could not see any path leading down onto the plains below, yet he could clearly see the glint of the vehicle windscreen far out on the plain.

Simon was sure that the entrance they came in was from the north and he knew that no way down existed for at least several kilometres north. Without hesitation, he started walking south, in the hope of finding a path down before darkness.

His water supply had finished. Ignoring the hunger pangs and incredible thirst, Simon continued for two hours. Luck then intervened and he spotted a spur which ran from the escarpment in front of his path. Several massive rock slides had made access possible onto the plain. Immediately he swung onto the spur and the first available path down. Slipping and sliding he cut himself on his way down to the plain below, oblivious of the abrasions and pain, blinded by his determination. Without stopping and with his adrenalin taking over, Simon continued on over the plains. Small streams afforded him the desperate water his body so needed to drink and wash the blood from his cuts.

The light began to fade as darkness took over. The moon was high and offered him some light even though his eyes had trouble focusing. Simon was now exhausted and weak with hunger. Unsure if he was even heading in the right direction as no landmarks were visible, he kept moving forward, tumbling over objects in the dark, twice crossing crocodile-infested rivers, startling dangerous buffalo, but never giving up.

Glancing at his watch it read midnight. He knew he had either passed the vehicle position or unwittingly been circling, as was often the case when no visible landmark was available to focus on. Time was running out and if he did not get to a phone by morning, it might be too late.

Hoping to be walking in a straight line, Simon needed to find the track they originally came in on. For another hour he stumbled along, growing weaker and weaker but knowing that he could not stop. He knew that somehow he had missed the track and was lost. In the morning, he would climb a rise and get his bearing. Looking for a place to rest, he located a stream and decided to cross, coming up on the bank opposite. As he reached the top he almost cried; there was the vehicle and he had possibly walked past it for hours!

He found the keys and gratefully, it started first try. Swinging the vehicle east onto the track, he fought to keep his eyes focused in the headlights as he picked his way down the road; trying enough in daylight, let alone in the headlights of a vehicle.

Several times he had to stop as exhaustion overcame him. It had been nearly forty-eight hours without sleep and his body cried out to stop. He fought hard to stay awake, splashing cold water over his face. Peering into the darkness resulted in a throbbing headache, splitting his senses; the faces of Dee and Priscilla spurring him on. He would not let them die.

A loud bang jolted Simon awake. He had slipped into a deep sleep but thankfully his slow speed had saved him as the vehicle hit a tree. Inspecting the damage he was so pleased that luck was once again alongside of him; just a small dent in the bull bar, nothing serious. The shock of the accident awoke within him a newfound energy and he continued driving into the night. Shaking his head in disbelief, he saw several camp fires. Bewildered as to who would be so far out here, he pulled up at the first fire.

A black face with a wide grin appeared at the window, 'Hi Simon, you have big problem no?' George grinned at him.

Simon jumped out and hugged the embarrassed George, 'You old bastard! I've never been so glad to see you in my life!' Simon almost wept.

In his haze of exhaustion, Simon saw several smiling black faces and then slumped to the ground. He had endured far more than the average human and now lay defeated, surrounded by old George and several young men, all carrying rifles.

The sun had already reached midday before Simon awoke. Rubbing his gritty eyes he saw some Aboriginal men sitting around a campfire eating meat which was sizzling and spitting on the embers of a fire. He instinctively staggered towards the fire and cut a chunk of meat which he ate ravenously. Like most Aboriginals, no one spoke; even old George knew that Simon would tell them what happened when he was ready but George's instincts told him something bad had happened. The day before, for some unknown reason, old George felt that his old friend was in trouble, and rounding up some of his mob, had headed towards the

Escarpment Country. His group had camped in this spot some way away from the Escarpment Country, as their centuries-old suspicion and fear of the little people in the Debil Debil country made it impossible to take his group any closer.

Simon knew this and knew that if he told the truth, Dee and Priscilla would be doomed; instead, he explained the situation but deliberately missed out any mention or knowledge of the little people.

Even so, George's group stood wide-eyed, reluctant to enter the Escarpment Country. It was only after George and Simon goaded them by calling them "town Aboriginals and cowards", did three volunteers agree to accompany them to rescue Dee and Priscilla.

Simon, George and the three volunteers left the rest at camp, with orders to have food prepared and remain until their return; even if it took them a week. Those left behind were relieved that they did not have to go into country none of them knew anything about; most had not even ventured this far from town, as the trappings of houses and shops plus other services kept many from ever leaving the comfort of society and entering the harsh reality of their ancestors.

Simon noted that the closer they got to the Escarpment Country, the more terrified his crew became; even old George cradled his rusty old rifle and fidgeted constantly. Simon knew the old man was aware that he had had contact with the little people. How George knew, Simon did not know, but George had the uncanny ability to predict and sense situations that were about to take place. Simon had witnessed George's intuition on many occasions over the decades since he had known him and he knew that George *had* encountered the little people in an aggressive meeting many years before.

Darkness overcame them as they reached the spot where Simon had initially left the vehicle only a week previously. That week seemed like months ago. George suggested they camp by the vehicle and head off at daylight the following day. Simon and the others agreed. He was still worn out; another night's rest would invigorate him for the harsh climb ahead. Bringing Priscilla back would be one immense task and was going to certainly tax the strength of all of them.

TEN

Dee sat for some time after Simon disappeared into the darkness. He knew that if Simon failed to make it, he and Priscilla would die. Dee felt strongly that waiting here would be a waste of time and that he needed to follow Simon's path and try to get the two of them out of the Escarpment Country to the plain below, and water. He might find fish or some means of food below but up here in this unforgiving territory, they had no chance.

Priscilla's ankle and now her leg were badly swollen and any movement was agonising. Unfortunately, along with everything else, the first-aid kit had also gone. As daylight began to rise, Dee tenderly picked up Priscilla and gamely started to walk over the uneven surface; astounded at the inhospitable terrain he faced. It was painfully slow and punishing.

At one stage, he was even tempted to throw Priscilla's camera away which she had slung around her neck. Two water canteens swinging from his shoulders seemed bad enough, but he knew that if they survived, even though the blood sample was gone, this would be the only evidence of their find. As the sun rose the heat became a furnace, no breeze existed and they gulped an ever diminishing supply of water. Dee placed Priscilla in a small hollow out of the direct sun and crumpled beside her, his tongue swollen and his throat dry; even the small sips of water he allowed himself failed to make any difference. Dee knew that Priscilla was slipping in and out of consciousness. Lack of food and not enough water made her breath come in small gasping motions.

At a guess, Dee thought it would be about midday. Looking back he nearly cried with despair; they had only come a short distance from the rise and he could clearly see the spot they had left hours before! Despondent, Dee decided to try and press on as he knew this could be their burial chamber and their bones would never be found if they succumbed to the elements and the grave position they now found themselves in.

He began to reflect on his life and felt shame wash over him. He had led a privileged life and admitted that he had always been one to put his own interests first, like most he thought, or was he trying to assuage his guilt? Looking down at Priscilla, he knew he was in love, possibly for the very first time and made a vow, that if somehow, they miraculously survived, he would marry her, if she would have him, and lead a less selfish lifestyle.

Picking up Priscilla's limp body, he attempted to continue, but after only a short distance, extreme weariness overcame him. The relentless heat of the sun was too much and he looked around desperately for a place with some shelter. Again he gently placed Priscilla down and sat beside her. Dee held Priscilla in his arms making her as comfortable as possible, as he lovingly and gently fed her small sips of water from the nearly empty canteen.

Night enveloped them and the chill bit into their bones. The rock they sheltered under thankfully still held warmth from the day's heat as the two lovers tried to sleep. A sense of utter despondency swept over Dee and as he held Priscilla close, tears ran down his face. Dee Fuller had given up. He waited for death to deliver peace to them. Here, in this timeless land that he had often visited and now found love so far from his homeland, Dee accepted their fate.

Dee would remember this night over the coming years as the longest in his life. Several times cramp hit his dehydrated body and painfully he would have to stand up and stamp his feet to stop the agony.

Priscilla spoke to him in shallow whispers between bouts of wakefulness; crying and apologising for her stupidity but with each whisper, Dee managed to placate her with his wit, by telling her that if they must die, then he would choose no other person to enter the next life with but her.

Drifting in and out of a troubled sleep, Dee awoke to the cry of a dingo pack on the hunt. His body was racked with thirst and hunger and he wondered why the pack was up on the escarpment when game was so flush below. Priscilla was still breathing shallowly and lay on the ground, curled in the foetal position. She too had given up all hope of rescue, even if Simon had made it, it would be another two days before rescue came and they still had to be found.

Dee was sure he was starting to hallucinate as figures moved before his eyes. Shaking his head, the scene became clearer and taking a deep breath he saw, standing before them, at least seven little people, including the young girl they had treated. Dee's heart began to palpitate as saw three men near him clutching a handful of spears. Grabbing hold of Priscilla, he held her close as he waited for the sound of a spear thudding into them.

With his eyes shut tight, Dee heard enlivened chatter and opened his eyes to see three backpacks being dropped onto the ground in front of them. Wide-eyed and terrified, Dee watched as the rifles were lowered onto the backpacks followed by a leg of recently cooked wallaby. Picking up the meat, Dee tore into the juicy flesh, breaking off small pieces for Priscilla who now sat up and grinned weakly at her new friend who carefully passed Priscilla some water.

Dee and Priscilla ate voraciously and coughed and gulped as they drank the water. The group consisted of three men, two old, one younger, two women, one with a child and the girl Priscilla had nursed. Standing silently, they watched with expressionless faces as Dee and Priscilla ate the offering and washed it down with fresh water. Then without a sound, they walked off into the morning light, as silently as they had arrived.

Dee opened the backpack and immediately turned on the satellite phone. He got a signal immediately and dialled 000, giving the operator their GPS coordinates! The operator seemed puzzled as to how and why they found themselves in such a predicament. About ten minutes later, the operator rang back and informed them that the Numbulwar police had advised that a helicopter would be dispatched from the Numbulwar area, as one was working nearby with the Aboriginals burning areas east of their position. The relief felt by Dee and Priscilla was immense, as they knew that only a short time before, they were preparing themselves to surrender to a slow and agonising death.

Dee hurriedly opened the first-aid kit and found Panadol Forte of which he gave two to Priscilla. She gratefully swallowed them whilst Dee cleaned up and bandaged her puffed up ankle. With renewed vigour, Dee found matches and lit a fire, purposely throwing green leaves on it to create a spiral of smoke. As they avidly watched the smoke make its way up into the air, the beat of a helicopter could be heard fast approaching on the horizon.

They laughed and cried as the machine circled above them looking for a safe area to land. Dry, red dust rose in a cloud as the pilot landed. After shutting the machine down, he alighted and approached the dishevelled pair.

'What the bloody hell are you two doing here?' he exclaimed.

'Looking for new plant species,' laughed Dee almost hysterically.

Shaking his head, the pilot assisted Priscilla into the front seat, Dee hopped into the back with the backpacks and rifles; the pilot wound the machine up and lifted into the blue sky.

'Can you go left a little please and keep low? We have some friends coming to possibly pick us up,' Priscilla requested.

'Yep, saw them a few minutes ago, nearly at the

escarpment. I'll drop over them and you can let them know you're with me,' replied the pilot.

In five minutes, Dee and Priscilla hovered over the group below. Simon recognised Priscilla as a backpack came crashing to the ground, the chopper powering away towards Nhulunbuy and hospital for Priscilla.

Simon picked up the pack and saw that it was his. Inside he found his phone wrapped tightly in a jumper. Switching it on, he soon found it ringing with Dee informing him that "friends" had returned their gear and that he even had Simon's rifle! Dee suggested Simon meet them in Darwin as soon as he could wrap up his camp and then all would be explained.

Simon could not believe that the unbelievable had happened. Together with his grateful crew, he turned around and headed back to the vehicle; his helpers more than a little happy to turn tail with apprehensive glances at what they would have had to enter.

The two patients succumbed to the rhythm of the helicopter and dozed, waking occasionally to look below at the vast expanse of wilderness that passed beneath them. They flew over small settlements, many with airstrips; the pilot informing them that most of them had never been lived in. Once again, Priscilla and Dee learned about how they had been built during a period when it was believed many Indigenous people wished to return to their homelands.

Hours later, as they approached the Nhulunbuy airstrip, an ambulance waited below to transfer them to the local hospital and treatment. Adrenalin kicked in and they now felt safe. As they landed, Dee gave Priscilla a warm smile and a tap on the shoulder; their ordeal was over.

The pilot landed near the ambulance and as the rotors slowed to a halt, Priscilla was transferred to a bed trolley by two smiling staff. Shaking the pilot by his hand, Priscilla mentioned to him that she knew that the helicopter was privately owned, and that she would pay all costs; much to the pilot's surprise. Collecting the address of the owners from the pilot, Dee worked out the number of hours it had taken and what the owners charged per hour. In fact, on arrival at the hospital, while Priscilla was being attended to, Dee, at her instruction, phoned the company, obtained the bank details and promptly paid the fee, plus an extra one thousand dollars in gratitude of the prompt service and skill of the pilot delivering them to safety.

Dee booked into the motel they had stayed at previously, showered and returned to the hospital to find Priscilla with her ankle in plaster, sound asleep. Looking at her, she looked so beautiful. Dee knew that he was in love and was so grateful that they had again found each other. Their ordeal had displayed a great test of compatibility which they had both passed with flying colours!

Settling into the chair by the bed, Dee nodded off, only waking for staff who supplied him coffee and food. Dee mused, smiling to himself; even hospital food tasted good! He reminded himself of his commitment to be a better person if he survived and he intended to keep the pledge.

The following morning, two local police arrived to take a statement. Dee and Priscilla stuck to the story that they had been documenting plant life in the escarpment area when the accident occurred. The two officers found it hard to believe that they had even managed to reach such a remote location. Dee went on to tell them that local safari operator, Simon Black, had dropped them off a few days prior and had arranged to pick them up and in actual fact, was on the way to do so. This appeared to satisfy the police who, when advised that no public monies had been expended in the rescue, were more than happy to close the case.

Once they'd left, Dee rang Simon who was back at his camp packing up for the season after a decent night's rest and relayed what he had told the police. Simon was pleased and the two men agreed it would be wise to wait until they met in Darwin to discuss their discovery and whether or not to make any statements, if at all. Dee and Priscilla had talked at length that it would be in the best interests of the little people to keep the encounter confidential. The number of little people they had met was insufficient for survival and so why speed up the process; simply let these Stone Age people who were so feared, disappear from the earth with dignity.

For two days Dee sat next to Priscilla's bed. She was making remarkable progress and they chatted for hours, careful not to mention their encounter with the little people if staff walked into the room. On her third day, with the help of a walking stick and Dee's help, Priscilla boarded a plane to Darwin to meet up with Simon.

Once in Darwin, Dee and Priscilla took a taxi into the city and Dee booked them into a hotel overlooking the harbour. Savouring the luxury, they gave the staff plenty of exercise delivering all types of delicious food to the room. After their ordeal, life took on a whole new meaning. Priscilla managed to hobble into town and buy some new clothes, visited a hair salon and to her absolute surprise and delight, was ushered by Dee into a jewellery shop. Beaming from ear to ear, Priscilla left the shop wearing a sparkling engagement ring.

That evening, they took a taxi to Simon's house and as they made their way up the path, Simon and his wife came out to meet them. Priscilla broke down and hugged Simon, thanking him for all that he had done and the super human effort he had endured to try and save her and Dee.

Since the rescue, the two parties had myriad questions to ask and over dinner, chatted late into the night. Simon was absolutely stunned about their meeting with the little people and Priscilla was so grateful to old George and his tribal members for coming to her rescue.

After a long dialogue, they were united in their decision to never disclose the adventure. One thing was certain, any kind of disclosure would mean the area being inundated with experts, who undoubtedly would destroy the life and hasten the demise of the little people. It was a unanimous vote that the little people would be far more happy living the balance of their lives as they had done for centuries.

Priscilla paid Simon handsomely, even though he objected saying that was his job, albeit an unusual one! Priscilla insisted.

She had more than satisfied her curiosity even though she intended not to prove her late father's theory for many reasons. In her own mind she had fulfilled her task and proved his theory. *Let sleeping dogs lie*, she thought. The indoctrination of the nation on certain aspects of society is better left alone, for what would she achieve, apart from vilification, like her dear father.

ELEVEN

Over breakfast the following morning, Dee and Priscilla agreed that out of everyone, old George, with his uncanny ability to sense their danger, would have eventually reached them with Simon and would have experienced tremendous effort to do so.

Priscilla remembered George wishing that he had a "good" vehicle, even though Dee reckoned it would be wrecked in a year! They wanted to do the right thing and recognise the care and effort that the old man had given them.

Although still in plaster, Priscilla and Dee decided to buy a vehicle and fill it with goods that George and Mary would appreciate. Dee would drive it to Numbulwar, deliver it with thanks, and catch a plane back to Darwin with Priscilla, then on home at last to Sydney.

Priscilla rang for a taxi and asked the driver to take them to a used car yard that they had seen on the way in from the airport; she recalls seeing a good selection of four-wheel drives. Pulling up outside the Toyota yard, they immediately bought a Toyota Troop carrier which was only three years old and in good condition. They paid for the vehicle and registered it in George's name. They then spent the rest of the day buying towels, crockery, and electrical items, returning to the hotel that evening with a stack of goods which filled the rear of the vehicle.

They were so excited the next day, driving down the Stuart Highway to deliver the vehicle to George in Numbulwar.

Priscilla was glad the vehicle they had purchased for George had air conditioning. Although it was the end of October, the wet season and build-up had already commenced; it was hot and sultry with plenty of cloud. The wet season could start early.

The journey down was pleasant and leisurely. Darwin had expanded since Dee's first visit years before; it was now a bustling city spreading south along the highway to Katherine.

'You know Dee; this trip has truly changed my perspective on Aboriginal Australia. I believe the full-bloods really have no say in their lives or future. It's now a big industry with too many vested interests; a real money-making exercise for hundreds of people manipulating the whole thing,' said Priscilla frowning, looking at Dee.

'My darling girl,' Dee replied. 'Unfortunately, like so many other issues in our so-called democratic society, nothing is too democratic and we really have no say in anything. I try hard not to think too much on any subject because in reality, we, the ordinary people, have no say.'

'God that sounds awful Dee, what exactly do you mean?' Priscilla asked.

'Well Priscilla, let's take your politicians who strut the halls of Canberra; do they really represent those who vote them in? I suggest not; they actually follow party lines, often in complete opposition to what the voter wants. The same you see for the Aboriginals; despite all the rhetoric, people who would or may have never seen a real Aboriginal, sit in some office in Canberra and decide the future for Indigenous people up here,' Dee responded trying not to get emotional and angry.

'Oh Dee, it all sounds so futile,' lamented Priscilla.

'Unfortunately my love, unless we have an Arab uprising, the status quo will remain the same and realistically this is not going to happen, so I intend to enjoy the rest of my life with you my sweet and not worry too much about it!' Dee replied smiling and patting her on the knee.

'I know, I agree, but it's all a bit sad,' replied Priscilla sighing.

'If the average person knew the double dealing and spin of politicians, and I believe they are waking up to it, we would spill into the streets and riot. Your and our reserve banks are a good point in question; did you know we don't even own them? They are run by private bankers who have so many shares in all the major banks! Most of what we perceive in life or are led to believe is actually false,' huffed Dee.

'Hell Dee, let's stop this! It's all too morbid. We'll deliver this to George and Mary and I just have to give the old bugger a big hug; no one's ever gone out of their way for me in my life. Of course, apart from you lover,' laughed Priscilla punching him affectionately.

They stopped at Katherine for a coffee and fatigue hit

them. The last few days had been tiring and all the stress of the expedition was catching up.

Dee suggested stopping at the beautiful Mataranka Springs for a day and stay overnight in the motel. It was a full day to Numbulwar from there and Priscilla agreed readily. They spent the remainder of the afternoon lounging on the banks of the crystal clear springs. Dee went for a splash while Priscilla in her leg cast, sat on the sidelines enjoying lively exchange with the few straggling "grey nomads" still filtering through on their way south.

After their evening meal in the motel restaurant, it was easy for them to fall asleep.

Traffic was light the next morning as they headed towards Roper Bar. They left early, just as the sun was beginning to rise. They made good time, enjoying the countryside which was mostly cattle stations with herds of Branham cattle grazing for miles.

Reaching the Roper River store at lunchtime, Dee filled with fuel and grabbing a cold drink, they decided to keep going. Turning off at Nukar, another Indigenous community, they headed north. There were no fences and wild buffalo, pigs and horses appeared as they sped along the dirt road. It was still in good condition and would remain so until the big rains arrived when whole sections would wash away.

They were so pleased when at last they arrived at Numbulwar. They drove straight to George and Mary's house. Dee smiled. Old George was sitting by a small fire smoking in front of the house. No one was more surprised when

Priscilla and Dee stepped out of the vehicle! Old George got to his feet and Mary appeared with a massive grin on her face. Priscilla took George by surprise and rushed up to him to give him a bear hug, thanking him so much for all that he had done for them.

Holding out the keys, Dee told George that the vehicle was for him and Mary and the goods inside were just another big "thank you" from them. The smile on the faces of their dear Aboriginal friends was something they would never forget. Priscilla sat down with George while Mary and Dee carted all the goods into the home they shared.

On entering their home, Dee was taken aback by the condition; it had been trashed, and the older couple did not even have cups or any crockery at all. A dilapidated mattress lay on the floor in the main bedroom and a badly damaged table in the kitchen, no power existed in the home. At first glance, it would seem that George and Mary existed on takeaways and tea boiled in a badly distorted can that George tended over the fire, on what was, the front yard.

Having booked a flight out on the Aboriginal air carrier the following morning, Dee faced a predicament; with no accommodation for visitors in town, he would have to show Priscilla the interior of the house and make plans promptly. Calling Priscilla into their home her reaction was one of shock initially, until she calmed down and turning towards George, asked him, 'George, is there a shop or store in town that sells mattresses and what time does it close?'

'Shop open til five o'clock and they sell all stuff,' he replied.

'Okay. We'll stay here if that is alright with you George and we'll go and get some food and a mattress. Is that okay?' asked Priscilla looking at George.

'No problems but we have sometimes big trouble here of a night,' George replied.

'After what I've been through George, big problems do not bother me! Come on Dee, let's do a store visit,' Priscilla replied heading towards the vehicle.

Mary went with them to the store and they bought a mattress, plus a good supply of groceries. Dee and Priscilla noticed that there were few people on the streets but several packs of flea-bitten dogs, most with skin and hair problems.

Back at George's home, Dee and Priscilla gave the house a good sweep before setting up the mattress in a spare room using the sheets and pillows they had bought in Darwin. Dee set up a small gas cooker and began cooking some freshly bought meat. Mary and Priscilla set the table, although they would have to stand to eat as for some bizarre reason, all the chairs had been destroyed.

The four friends then sat around the campfire in front of the home and sipped coffee and tea in the new mugs. It was during this quiet time, that Dee and Priscilla managed to find out why the old couple had no possessions. It appeared that although they owned many tracts of land and collected a pension, the younger members of the community continually harassed and threatened the elders for money.

Dee and Priscilla found it hard to believe but had no reason to not believe them. George and Mary made it quite clear their hatred for alcohol and drugs and the negative effect it had on Indigenous communities. George told them that he'd phoned the police so many times but even they eventually were overwhelmed.

As darkness fell and they watched the dancing light of the flames, Dee and Priscilla heard and felt, the community coming alive. Loud voices of people arguing and walking by made them uneasy. George suggested they go inside after one particularly noisy group went past, obviously high on alcohol or drugs.

Sitting on the floor around a small battery lantern Dee and Priscilla had with them, their conversation interrupted as they listened to the noise that spilled onto the dusty streets.

'This goes on every night; it gets real bad,' said old George gravely.

At about ten o'clock after a final cup of tea, they decided to try and turn in for the night. Just as they rose to get up, several loud knocks were made on the door.

'Go away!' screamed George. 'I'll call police!'

'Open up old man! We want some money to buy gunja,' a voice screamed from outside.

George picked up a mobile phone to call the police just as the door burst open and three youths burst in, one brandishing a nulla-nulla. In one swift movement, Dee grabbed the intruder, yanking the weapon off him and ejected him out the door. Mary and George were shouting at the other two who bolted at the sight of Dee now brandishing the weapon, ready to defend Priscilla and his two elder Aboriginal friends.

'Incredible! I had no idea,' said Priscilla shocked, as she hugged Mary who was still shaking.

'Big problems all the time, elders now have no say; the young ones threaten and bash us all the time,' replied George sadly.

No other intrusion occurred during the long night but screams and fighting continued until daylight. Dee and Priscilla snatched a few hours' sleep, feeling so sorry for their elderly friends. Priscilla kept shaking her head and voicing angrily that no one should have to live that way.

They understood why George wanted to move north to his country, away from all the problems here.

'George, after the wet season, I'll send a truck in with a small demountable for you and Mary so you can escape to your land north of here when you feel like it. Now please, do not let anyone use your vehicle; only yourself,' advised Priscilla sternly.

The night's events had shocked and disturbed Dee and Priscilla, and as they boarded the plane later that morning, the wellbeing of their dear friends played heavily on their minds. A worried frown on Priscilla's face portrayed her concern as she saw her two old friends standing by their new vehicle. She watched them waving until they disappeared from view.

'Dee, I had no idea just how dysfunctional the community is,' blurted Priscilla, still in shock as the plane levelled out for the flight to Nhulunbuy.

'Tragically a lot of them are the same,' replied Dee.

He sneered as he continued, 'Despite all the experts and money thrown at the problem, it's simply getting worse.'

'No one seems to have an answer. Well, at least I can help George and Mary; such a lovely old couple,' mumbled Priscilla.

The two-hour journey to Nhulunbuy seemed to take forever and before they landed at the Nhulunbuy airport – their on-flight was only half an hour away – they transferred for the flight to Darwin. Sleep overpowered them for the entire flight to Darwin, only waking when the hostess informed them they had only minutes before landing.

Back in "civilisation" was a great relief; the night before seemed so far removed from what the ordinary Australian enjoyed. Priscilla was more than disturbed at the life her new friends had to endure and she promised herself to at least try and do something to give George and Mary a more peaceful and content lifestyle. Settling again into the hotel overlooking the Darwin Esplanade, neither felt like an evening meal; the past two days had not turned out to be the relaxing drive and overnight they'd anticipated; quite the contrary. It had been traumatic and upsetting, especially for Priscilla who had only wished to thank her would-be rescuer George, and repay the old man for his incredible kindness.

The following day, Priscilla and Dee met Simon and his wife in the city for lunch. Priscilla reiterated her gratitude to the safari operator who had gone beyond the call of duty in unusual circumstances; not one's average safari! In his usual style, Simon dismissed her glowing tributes, just thrilled that all had turned out well as it could have so easily gone horribly wrong; he dare not think what could have resulted if the satellite phone had not been returned or old George had not saved him!

Unaware that Priscilla and Dee had travelled back to Numbulwar with gifts for George and Mary, when they learned of their story, Simon and his wife had to agree, albeit sadly, that yes, George would give in to constant humbugging and all the goods taken to him and Mary, including the vehicle, would be lost, stolen or wrecked within a month.

The four then went their own ways and Dee and Priscilla returned to the hotel for their last night in Darwin. Their direct flight to Sydney was leaving the following morning at 6.00am.

TWELVE

Priscilla gazed below as the aircraft banked slowly to line up for the landing in Sydney; a feeling of sadness embraced her. Her trip had far from ended the way she'd imagined. Yes, some would say it had been highly successful and the knowledge and discovery made were far beyond her wildest expectations, but for Priscilla it dug deep and it depressed her to think that the small group of people they had miraculously stumbled upon, would die out and most likely, in her lifetime – centuries of living in the Escarpment Country by the little people – gone. What was eating her up was the fact that the knowledge she now possessed was invaluable but she was impotent to do anything about it.

The evening with George and Mary had affected her deeply. She was shattered at their dysfunctional society. *Whose fault was it? Is each society accountable for its own functioning? Had the breakdown of normality and total lack of respect for the elders resulted from the introduction of certain negative aspects of western lifestyle?* Priscilla noted a certain lack of direction in the younger members of the community and felt somewhat responsible. *In trying to help them, had we, in fact, caused the problems? Would a new direction, for example, tough love, improve the situation or was it too late?* Shaking her head from side to side, she knew deep down that no one had the definitive answer.

Collecting their baggage, Dee and Priscilla were mutual in their reflective mood. They were pleased to be back but something was amiss, and instead of the triumphant homecoming, they appeared defeated and deflated, finding it hard to come to terms with all that had taken place. *Was it really only a few weeks ago?*

Priscilla's plaster cast was removed a few weeks later and they were back to enjoying long walks and quiet times together. They spent many hours making love, their bodies in tune with the needs of each other.

Dee suggested they get married and have a proper wedding and invite a few friends. Priscilla agreed. It would be an opportune distraction which the two lovers badly needed; their melancholy refusing to unveil itself. Neither discussed the trip much but it hung over them like a pall of smoke, relentless and disturbing. Even in her sleep, Priscilla was haunted by the face of the small stone-age girl she had so delicately nursed; her eyes and face. Many nights she woke up in a sweat; it began to haunt her.

Dee and Priscilla faced the reality that as far as friends went in Australia, few, if any, existed. Dee being American, he only knew Simon Black and his wife, a couple of American friends and one from the UK. That was it really. He knew they would attend but apart from them, he admitted that because of his nomadic lifestyle over the last few years, making real friends had been almost impossible.

Priscilla agreed. She had lived and worked in the UK all her life and had no Australian friends. She knew of only two who would make the journey from the UK to their wedding.

Setting a date, they posted off invitations. Priscilla bought two plane tickets and placing two hundred dollar notes in the envelope, sent an invitation to George and Mary, requesting them to come a week earlier so that she and Dee could show them the sights of Sydney.

This small gesture cheered them up immensely and they set about preparing for the wedding. They looked forward to the company of George and Mary and hearing the stories they loved to tell of their past.

Despite not hearing from George or Mary, it was with great expectation that Dee and Priscilla eagerly awaited in Arrivals for the elderly couple. Clasping a bunch of colourful flowers, Priscilla started to shed a few tears, as first off the plane, guided by a smiling air hostess, were George and Mary, both looking a tad bewildered as they appeared down the walkway.

Embracing the confused but beaming couple, Priscilla and Dee felt honoured that these two special people had made the trip so far from their own country. They guided them to the baggage collection area after George and Mary had made a bathroom call.

George and Mary seemed to be enjoying the attention bestowed on them by their hosts and chatted incessantly while the baggage collection began. Dee stood with George as they waited for their luggage and it was only after everyone else had collected their bags that it dawned on Priscilla and Dee that *neither* had any luggage. Priscilla felt a little embarrassed; of course she should have known that all the old couple had was half a packet of cigarettes and the clothes they were wearing. It was on the way to the car that the situation with the non-existent baggage hit Dee and Priscilla and they looked at each other and had a good chuckle.

Priscilla suggested that on the way home, they stop at the RM Williams store and buy them some new clothes. They agreed wholeheartedly, trying to take in the sights as they sped along in the car. George did request a stop at a grocery store to purchase some cigarettes although Priscilla didn't like the idea of supplying cigarettes to her old friends but relented and ran into a small corner shop returning with a carton of Winnies Red, the favourite smoke of the couple. Priscilla reminded herself not to judge others too harshly. She had tried her utmost to kick the habit but found it extremely taxing. Her Indigenous friends enjoyed their rellies, so who was she to deny them or criticise.

Dee assisted George whilst Priscilla helped Mary try on an array of clothing. The foursome left the store some time later, with George looking resplendent in a new Akubra and several sets of shirts and trousers. Mary chose skirts and shirts and was beaming with pride in her new outfit while carrying a bag with additional clothing. Not yet finished, their hosts guided them into Kmart and new panties, bras and underpants were added to the shopping. Priscilla was in her element guiding her guests around and it was late in the evening when the four returned to Priscilla's home via the Sydney Harbour Bridge.

Dee had bought some juicy steaks to cook for dinner and Priscilla suggested to her guests that if they wished to shower prior to dinner, there was plenty of time. George and Mary confessed to being tired and they unanimously agreed on a good night's sleep.

Priscilla found an old suitcase and packed it with their new clothes and put their old clothes into the washing machine. She returned to the bedroom and laid the bed back ready for her two tired but very special guests.

They enjoyed the fruits of Dee's cooking and then retired to bed. What a wonderful, eventful day it had been and Dee and Priscilla were delighted to have two such admired guests in their home, ready to celebrate their wedding in three days' time.

The next two days were spent soaking up the sights of Sydney and of course, some more shopping! Sadly, Priscilla found out that the new vehicle she had supplied George and Mary was wrecked between Katherine and Numbulwar. George had relented and loaned the vehicle to a cousin. Another lesson learnt for Priscilla – personal possessions did not feature in the Indigenous culture. For generations, tribes had shared all possessions and food; to even consider altering this unique feature would be inherently wrong. Western society could learn so much by taking on board some of the traditions of this ancient people; personal greed and corruption being endemic in western culture.

Priscilla warmed even more to her guests during the two-day period; their simplistic outlook on life and total hatred of alcohol because of the devastating result of overuse by their people, bonded Priscilla closer to George and Mary. They were people with morals, struggling in the modern world, overwhelmed by a society so foreign to the past of their people.

****

On a beautiful, warm spring day, Priscilla Ashton-Jones and Dee Fuller, stood facing each other on the green lawns running down to Sydney Harbour, with the bridge rising majestically in the background, whilst a celebrant married the happy couple. Proudly standing next to them were their attendants; George and Mary who had accepted the role with warmth and happiness at being chosen for such an important job! Ceremony over, the happy couple kissed to cheers from the small crowd of friends and family from many parts of the world. Simon Black and his wife had attended, stopping briefly in Sydney on their way to America to attend a safari show in California, in order to book clients for the next season.

It was with heavy heart that Dee and Priscilla farewelled their friends the following morning, with George and Mary promising to visit them again as soon as possible. Dee and Priscilla returned home to pack for their honeymoon in Broome, West Australia. They couldn't wait to get to Cable

Beach and spend a week just relaxing and enjoying each other's company.

Grateful to have the house to themselves again, they shared a light meal before retiring to bed in readiness for the early rise the following morning. Priscilla was really looking forward to their trip to Broome, neither having ever visited the area. She had decided on Broome for the simple fact that an acquaintance had a job on an Aboriginal settlement south of Broome and she wished to visit it during their stay. Their experience in Arnhem Land had triggered an interest in Indigenous Australia as they were concerned with the ongoing calamity, relevant in most Indigenous communities. Their aim would be to gather as much information firsthand as possible. George and Mary's problems would need dramatic and decisive action which no government would have the stomach to do; their answer would be to simply throw more money at the problem without any direction and which no doubt, initially triggered the issues.

Priscilla had a taxi booked for 5.00am the following morning and although tired, she and Dee woke several times during the evening and talked for hours. Dee was hardly surprised when deep in concentration, Priscilla expressed a strong desire to return to the escarpment area the following dry season to check on her patient. Her main concern was to bring closure to their nearly calamitous trip and to do this; she needed to know that the young girl had recovered.

Dee agreed in principle; they owed their lives to the Stone People of Arnhem Land, and so sipping hot Milo at three in the morning, a decision was made to return the following year to check on their "saviours" and with luck, give them some gifts in appreciation for the return of their property.

It'd been a long night. Showered and ready for the taxi, they helped load their cases into the boot. Dee liked chatting to taxi drivers and sat in the front, amusing Priscilla with their banter and listening to the taxi driver who seemed to have the answer to all the world problems.

After going through the usual routine, they boarded the flight and soon settled into their seats and slept; being woken by the hostess just before landing. Collecting the baggage and leaving the terminal in Broome to catch a cab to the resort they had booked into, the hot, humid air was stifling and they took relief in the air-conditioned cab for the short drive to Cable Beach. After booking in and unpacking, a walk on Cable Beach called to them. Walking north over the rocks, Priscilla giggled at the few late tourists who were still visiting this late in the season. The tourists were naked! The beach was a nudist beach and Dee immediately suggested that they join in as they had not brought their bathers. They stripped off and plunged into the delicious cold water.

'Dee! This is so liberating!' Priscilla shrieked as they splashed each other with water.

'Hmm and you look a real gorgeous spunk my love; just the way I like you,' laughed Dee.

After the trauma of the Arnhem Land trip, plus the wedding arrangements, and now with Priscilla's ankle healed, they felt that at last they truly could relax. They left the cool water and walked back to their clothes hand in hand. They sat on the warm sand to dry whilst watching the sun set in a blaze over the water. Dee felt caught up in the moment and hungrily pulled Priscilla to him, kissing her with deep passion and longing. He hastily glanced up and down the beach in the twilight, and spotting no one nearby, pushed Priscilla gently onto her back. Parting her legs, he entered in one swift motion, slipping into her wet vagina, still kissing her passionately. Soft groans wafted in the silent night air as their bodies rose to meet; each thrust relentless and more powerful than the other, building to a crescendo in a mind-blowing orgasm.

Rolling off and gasping for air, Dee and Priscilla held hands while looking at the stars above. They did not speak; they did not need to. They had found each other again and knew that only death would part them.

For three days the performance was repeated; swimming nude, making love and relaxing on the beach; all the world's problems forgotten as each sexual tryst became more intense, their orgasms more explosive. Without reservation, they became fine-tuned to the erotic wants of each other.

On the fifth day as planned, a friend and old associate from their London days, Kylie Jones, picked them up as planned and they drove the one hundred and eighty kilometres south to visit the community of Bidgydanga; a mission run originally run by the Catholic Church. Kylie then told them that the mission once ran a working station south of the settlement with big gardens and milking sheds. The station was now owned by Indigenous owners but the main area was not operating as a station and two other areas had been leased to other stations.

Arriving at the settlement reminded Dee and Priscilla of other communities they had visited; several people, mostly younger ones, wandered around haphazardly, rubbish and mangy dogs everywhere. The group visited the health centre and a well-stocked shop. The takeaway was closed because they were unable to get workers to keep it open, and several new homes were under construction. They learned from Kylie that the contractor responsible was, according to the contract, supposed to hire locals. Several had been bussed to Broome for training but even so, none turned up for work.

Dee and Priscilla found the people friendly and they chatted to a few at the swimming pool and shop. Everyone seemed happy enough but on questioning the issue of alcohol which was banned, it still remained a big problem. Somehow, somewhere, it was still available. Aware that it was a highly emotive topic, neither delved too deeply into the issue of Indigenous Australia as no one seemed to have any new ideas to improve life for communities. They soon gleaned that in fact, it was highly political and offensive to even discuss or mention the subject. Bizarrely, they appeared to be content that the system was dysfunctional and going nowhere. Kylie agreed that as far as she was concerned, her job was to help deliver health services and she, like all the workers, wanted to do their best despite everything. All they could do was offer their services until such time a new system was introduced.

That evening, Dee and Priscilla discussed the day in length and agreed how wonderful the many workers who lived in remote Aboriginal communities were. They often lived in trying circumstances yet did not hesitate in their wish to assist.

'Priscilla, maybe *we're* totally wrong about the whole thing. Why is it *us* who have to impose our will on Indigenous Australia? The full-bloods who live in remote areas deserve our assistance. The industry employs a lot of people and our recent experiences have certainly changed my mind on a raft of issues,' spoke Dee in solemn tones.

Priscilla nodded saying, 'Hmm, I agree. Maybe my father was a little *too* enthusiastic in his research, and to stir up trouble would do no one any good. Basically, all I see now is everyone trying to do the best they can, no one has the answer or an alternative.'

'True. I still suggest we head to Darwin and obtain a small dwelling for George and Mary, we did promise and we owe them that,' replied Dee.

THIRTEEN

Their stay in Broome certainly helped Priscilla and Dee become more settled and focused; their main concern for the Aboriginal members of the Australian community was a far bigger problem than they, as individuals, could rectify or help. George and Mary were their priority in supplying them with a new dwelling on their tribal land and even visiting them occasionally. They wanted to spend as much time as possible with this special couple.

On arrival in Darwin, they again stayed on the Esplanade whilst visiting a few building firms in search of a suitable dwelling for transport to the Gulf. One firm with experience suggested taking the chosen dwelling – a one-roomed shack of sturdy steel construction – as a flat pack and erecting it on stumps on site. Agreeing on a price, the owner advised that they had one in stock as well as a four-wheel drive truck available and they could deliver it the following week. The wet season had not started and the build-up would last another two months. If George agreed, then they would go ahead as planned.

Priscilla phoned George who was ecstatic; agreeing to meet them at the turnoff south of the settlement on the following Thursday. After the call, Priscilla was smiling; such a good feeling to help her friends. With the contract signed and the building paid for, Dee and Priscilla returned to the hotel, happy in the knowledge that they had kept their promise to George of his dream of a dwelling on his land.

A week later, Priscilla found herself sitting in her father's office; her mindset completely different to the last time she had sorted through a lifetime of dedication – some might even say bordering on obsession. Priscilla recognised that his infatuation on the subject of migration patterns in ancient Australia, in the end, really did not matter. Politically, no one was interested in any subject that was not "politically correct" and whatever dogma was preached by those in control ultimately became truth.

To pursue her father's path of proving that several early waves of humanity *had* entered the Australian continent was ineffectual, as he had soon discovered that powerful interests would denigrate and humiliate those who pursued such a path. With Dee's help, Priscilla packed her father's lifetime of work, even printing the pictures of the little people they had met, and placed them into the folder in the cartons. Several weeks passed and all the paperwork lying in the office had been meticulously documented and stacked into one of the spare rooms. Priscilla pondered whether, upon her death, anyone coming across this information would be able to take up the research as by then, any evidence or proof would most likely have disappeared into history.

Dee suggested that with the volatile world they lived in, another wave of humanity could possibly make its way into

Australia, thereby nullifying the present debate.

With the exploding population on the planet, it was not beyond the realms of possibility that in decades to come, the Indigenous population, despite all the indignity shown by those shouting racism and more funding, ceases to exist. The mindset of those who control the seat of power in Canberra might change if an invasion of millions of starving people entered the country.

Priscilla and Dee decided to close this chapter in their lives and take advantage of their financial success. They did not want for much; just each other's company, and to travel and enjoy themselves was their decision. Priscilla had been informed that the dwelling had been erected on George and Mary's land and the contractor had, as instructed, placed a double bed, and table and chairs in the dwelling.

The news brought closure for Priscilla but she told Dee that she had one more wish to fulfill. She still wanted to return to the escarpment area and visit the caves to see if any trace of the little people was present and if possible, beyond her wildest dreams, find them again.

Priscilla knew the helicopter company would drop them off in the same spot they had been rescued; Dee had kept the coordinates and they knew from there, the entrance to the cave sites was only an hour or two away in a westerly direction. Priscilla and Dee then settled down into the tranquil life of a married couple; gardening and enjoying musical events.

Simon called in on his way home from America and stayed for the weekend. They talked long into the night and he too, agreed that trying to change anything seemed impossible; far better to let matters pan out the way they were heading.

Simon was rather surprised that they'd decided to again visit the Escarpment Country and reminded them to keep control of the satellite phone and keep him informed of their whereabouts!

For some unknown reason, Priscilla spent many a long night unable to sleep; she kept seeing the little people walking off into the mist. It began to overwhelm her and on many occasions, she had to wake up Dee as she began to fear her obsession.

Unable to rid the image of the forlorn-looking figures slowly fading away, Dee came to the conclusion, as she had, that the backpacks and rifle had been a burden to them and that they had returned them having been shown kindness, possibly for the first time ever. History had proven that for centuries they had had to fight to survive in the harsh stone country and as nomads, their only weapons were spears which were used for their hunter-gatherer existence. Most of Priscilla's working life had been spent studying ancient mankind; long since gone into the annals of history. Meeting the little people had had such a strong influence on Priscilla; more than she dared to admit and knowing that they still existed, and that she had interacted with this unique, ancient primitive tribe, filled her with sadness and a whirlwind of emotions.

Dee knew that however dangerous it was to revisit the

escarpment area, Priscilla would not get closure until she'd finished her quest, not for glory or gain but to satisfy her own desires to properly thank her special saviours. Surprisingly, Dee admitted that he too felt a need to return. Their chance meeting had affected both of them and the experience now seemed surreal. Unwittingly, Dee and Priscilla were drawn to something far greater than either perceived. They'd discussed and agreed that *not* to return would play on their minds for always. They had to follow their hearts and risk all, to once again stand on the same ground as the Stone People.

Some months passed and their passion to return to the Escarpment Country continued unabated; however, it was agreed to visit George and Mary first and spend some quality time with the elderly couple. In many of their conversations, Priscilla and Dee felt that few, if any, had ever really become so attached and held such a close relationship with Indigenous Australia, without imposing their own thoughts or really listened to the thoughts, dreams and opinions of the people themselves.

Priscilla had deep respect for her new friends and knew that if they spent some time with them, their thoughts could be strikingly different to those who chart the lives of Indigenous Australia. *Would they be able to understand why it was failing dramatically?*

Landing in Darwin, the wet season had not quite ended and they walked from the terminal, uncomfortable in the hot and sticky conditions. It was mid-afternoon and a storm was building to the west; small gushes of cooler air heralded the approaching storm. Returning to the car yard where they had originally bought George's Troopy, they decided on a cheaper, older model diesel Land Cruiser, making sure that the air-conditioner worked before paying for it! The rest of the afternoon was spent filling their two backpacks with dehydrated foodstuffs and other items, ready for their trip again into the interior after spending some precious time with George and Mary.

For two more days they remained in Darwin at the hotel they had used on previous occasions, stocked up with items for their friends and added to their own supplies for at least ten days. Dee and Priscilla chose *not* to tell George about their forthcoming trip as he would certainly only worry himself and they didn't wish to burden him; he would be mortified.

On the third day, they set off down the Stuart Highway towards Numbulwar. They were more excited with this trip than before, as they mutually agreed that life in Sydney, after a lifetime of travel, had become dull and monotonous.

After two days of driving they arrived outside George and Mary's home. The trip had been rugged as several sections of the road had suffered because of heavy monsoon rains. Even as they pulled up, the monsoon season was still active; thunder rattled around them and lightning streaked across the sky as heavy drops of rain beat down onto the car.

George and Mary had witnessed their arrival and waved madly for them to come inside; despite sprinting to the house they were drenched in the deluge.

No warmer a welcome had either ever received than that

from their hosts; beautiful big smiles in a genuine show of warmth! Later, Priscilla would remember it as likening it to coming home. For several hours they chatted while sipping sweet tea before retiring to bed. Nothing had changed much but the inclement weather at least kept troublemakers off the street.

The following morning after a lie in, the Land Cruiser was repacked, and like four enthusiastic children, they headed to George's tribal country. The men were looking forward to fishing, especially the barramundi which would be on the bite in such warm water!

FOURTEEN

During the trip north – although picking their way around suspect areas – they became bogged and had to use the winch to extract the vehicle. Priscilla commented many times how grateful they were to have bought a vehicle with a working winch. The plan to buy a vehicle that included a winch had not been remotely discussed, just sheer luck that the vehicle they chose included one and more pertinently, it worked!

By mid-afternoon they'd arrived at the shack they'd bought for George and Mary. Upon entering, they discovered that it hadn't been used. George told them that it was because they'd had no transport and the wet season had made it impossible for them to come out to his tribal country. Unpacking the provisions inside the home, they ventured down to the estuary to catch fresh fish for tea; the fish were in abundance as they swarmed in on the incoming tide.

After the crowds of Sydney, Priscilla and Dee unwound and absorbed the peace of the evening; hooking fish and chatting to their hosts. Over a scrumptious meal of fresh fish and sweet tea, the four friends sat under the stars and talked about many different subjects. Priscilla and Dee looked at each other in surprise when George, looking seriously at them, said, 'Do you really want to know what I think about the present problems of my people? No one has ever asked me or as far as I know, has asked any other Aboriginal that I know?'

Priscilla replied seriously, 'George, I'd be honoured to hear what you have to say. Please be honest and tell us what you really think.'

George lay back in the chair, the dancing flames of the camp fire showing an old man who had lived during a period of great change for his people. Drawing on his cigarette he started, 'You must remember, only a few decades ago my people roamed this land; we had different beliefs and a simple hunter-gatherer existence. I know if the British had not settled, what you called Australia, my land, then someone else certainly would have done. The constant wailing against the British is a waste of time and fanciful to those who think we would still have roamed this country as we always had done.'

George stopped for a sip of tea and lit another cigarette. Staring into the fire he continued. Priscilla and Dee sat enthralled and did not utter a word; their hearts pleading for this old man to continue and give them his most inner thoughts.

'Light skin, white fellas are accepted as Aboriginal. They only have to say they are Aboriginal and are accepted and they join the gravy train with their rants of racism, so I am only talking about *my* people, the full-blood, those flag-burning whites who claim us to be black trash and handicap genuine Aboriginal concerns. Our culture is tens of thousands of years old; how can we change in a short two hundred years?'

Sipping his tea and concentrating, George continued, 'It's

a joke now that the "experts" added Aboriginal language and culture into the schools; waste of time. We should be teaching our young something of value to them in the future in the modern world; they are pushing our advancement backwards by trying to be politically correct. We are in the computer age, the kids don't care about culture; watch them walking about aimlessly yakking on mobile phones, do they hunt? No bloody way; it's all takeaway. Most would get lost on the outskirts of town and no one lives there anyway.

'We only handicap our young by wasting their time on Stone Age culture. We're in the sophisticated age of computers and we have to embrace and advance; not go backwards if we want to advance into the future. White fellas don't want their kids taught how you lived centuries ago, it is stupid.'

Priscilla and Dee stared at each other, shocked. Here and now, sitting around a camp fire listening to an old man of ancient heritage, possibly speaking freely for the first time in his life about his true feelings, Priscilla was of the opinion that had this man of knowledge been asked his opinion, he may have been of more benefit to his people's dilemma than the hundreds of highly educated alleged white experts.

'The white fellas further intervened with great fanfare because of our child molestation as you call it and took away our social service payments. Then we had hungry, sexually abused children. It is our culture for older men to train younger women or girls and older women to train young men. Muslims marry girls as young as five and slice girl's vaginas, yet you let that practice continue in Australia. Look at the

Catholic Church; you did nothing about that yet you carry on about *our* traditions. You western people have child abuse as you call it but you do not understand our culture. It may be wrong but we don't understand this as it has been part of our ancient culture for centuries. We had no power structure, money or political ambitions or even a status ladder but simply tribal law, like your law. We may not have been perfect but it treated us well for centuries. I cannot see one feature of what is happening now to all full-blood Indigenous communities that is any better than what we had when I was a child; I think we had a much happier and fulfilled life back then. That is my say and I have finished.'

George sat with dignity. Was this the first time in his life that he had felt the freedom to speak his mind, tell it as he saw it, in a lifetime that saw him living the tribal life in comparison to that of a town-dwelling Aboriginal in a white-run community.

'George, one last question if I may? What do *you* see as the future for your particular community?' asked Priscilla solemnly.

After a short sigh, George replied, 'Unfortunately not good. We have no genetic tolerance to alcohol; is killing us slowly. To close down our isolated communities and try and integrate us into white society at this time would be devastating. I think the only thing to do is to try and have some type of tourist ventures on the millions of acres we own now, for white Australians. Let our young take older retired white Australia on fishing and camping trips and try and integrate slowly; the stupid schemes the governments waste millions on now simply do not work.'

'You could be right, but don't you think that most of the white people who run the communities are doing a good job?' Dee asked.

'Yeah, for sure, many are dedicated and treat us well but in the long run this must stop. We have to be taught more responsibility, especially our young ones; they're being taught the world owes them a living and it's their land and all they have to do is *take* all the time. This one day will stop and reality will be that we have to be more self-sufficient,' replied George.

Priscilla sighed, 'Well, we all agree that things will have to change but we all agree that no one seems to have the right answer. Let's go to bed; we're all tired and I want to explore tomorrow.'

'The white fella; he's funny really, telling us *he* stopped us from killing each other in our tribal skirmishes. Well, in my life, the white fella has killed millions of his own kind and still doing it today. I listen to the news; some say we make things up as we go along to help our situation. I tell you, all those white fellas in Canberra lie and bullshit every day; never heard one tell the truth yet,' commented old George who threw his head back and laughed, as did Priscilla and Dee. The wisdom of old George was something they'd never thought possible. Priscilla had completely changed her mind on Indigenous Australia and was sorry that her father had not spent more time with George and Mary; he might then have not become so wrapped up in his research. Yes, there probably had been several waves of early groups migrating to Australia but in the long term, did it really matter? Nothing in today's society was really as it was. Spin and deception had become the norm in all aspects of society; the truth, if at all, was something few in government or society were really interested in; "self-interest and greed" being their mantra.

Priscilla and Dee slept well that night; content in the simple surroundings they found themselves in and happy to be in the company of such a humble and uncomplicated couple yet far more sophisticated and conscious of Australian society and politics then they had ever imagined. They were overwhelmed at the apparent knowledge the old man George had accumulated in his lifetime. He had impressed them as they listened intently to all he had to say and in all cases, agreed with his view that *his* was a culture of co-existence with his fellow man, whereas white society thinks in terms of monetary penalties and reward.

Who were we to force our ways on to an unprepared race? Priscilla and Dee concurred how ridiculous it was to teach Aboriginal children to track goannas, when the majority ate at Macca's down the road. Far more sensible and logical to prepare them for the world they will have to co-exist in; that of the "white" society.

The days passed languidly with George and Dee hunting and fishing while Priscilla assisted Mary in collecting pandanus for basket-making, a pastime Mary really enjoyed as well as searching for mud crabs and spearing them.

Priscilla was staggered how Mary seemed to find the creatures hidden in rocks, simply by looking for tracks or a telltale bubble that the creature was present.

The four friends lived the highlife off the land; George even shot a buffalo and demonstrated how to remove the backstrap. He cut it razor thin, rolled the meat in flour and cracked pepper before cooking it in hot oil on the frying pan. Delicious!

Dee and Priscilla didn't want to leave and felt sad as their time drew nearer. Priscilla had arranged for a helicopter that was carrying out a survey out of Numbulwar, to drop them off in the Escarpment Country. Although she hadn't told George of their plans, she did suspect that he had some idea, yet never mentioned it. As a matter of fact, he never brought up the topic of his personal thoughts again either. He simply moved forward, enjoying the hunting and their traditional way of living.

Dee surmised that George *must* have seen the two backpacks left untouched in the back of the Land Cruiser. On the morning of their departure, George and Mary informed them that they wished to stay and asked Priscilla and Dee to call in at their home and ask their son who was living there, to come and pick them up later.

Priscilla told George that the Land Cruiser was his and that they would leave it with their son. Nothing was said as they knew that George would again lend it to all his relatives as was their tradition and way of life; personal possessions meant nothing to the full-blood Aborigine.

It was an unhappy parting and Priscilla shed a tear as she watched the older couple waving goodbye. What a great and inspiring time they had had with their friends and Dee and Priscilla promised to return but Dee knew that George and Mary had heard so many promises from "white people" that they actually did not expect them to fulfill it.

Arriving at the house that George and Mary lived in, the son and his partner came to the door, still half asleep. When informed, George's son told Dee to leave the vehicle at the airport and that he would pick it up later; as time was paramount, Dee agreed and promised to leave the keys under the spare tyre.

At the airport, the chopper pilot was already fuelling up, ready for take-off. Tossing the backpacks into the back, the pilot warned them that storms had been forecast and he was anxious to lift off and get going, as he was ferrying the machine *back* to Darwin for service and would drop them off on the way. They'd agreed that he would pick them up in seven days at the drop-off or earlier if they called him from the satellite phone.

As the helicopter lifted off, they felt apprehensive. The last time into the area had nearly cost them their lives; however, this time they were better prepared and the drop-off was not far from their ultimate destination. Placing the earphones over their heads, they chatted to the pilot, Trevor, as wild rivers and wetlands passed majestically under them.

'Have you guys got permits?' asked the pilot casually.

'To be honest, no,' Dee replied. 'We came to spend time

with George and Mary at their coastal camp and forgot.'

'Don't worry, only *I* actually know you're here. I'll tell the boss when I hit Darwin,' laughed Trevor.

Priscilla's heart skipped a beat as the sheer cliff face of the Escarpment Country came into view; dark clouds swirled above as the menacing storm approached.

'Are you sure you folks will be okay?' Trevor asked worryingly.

'No problems. There are a few caves close by we can shelter in. I'm sure it won't last long; at least water will not be a problem this time,' answered Dee.

'I'll have to head north and skirt around this one,' said Trevor, 'and I'll keep my phone on for your call. I'll be back in six days anyhow to finish the audit on some of the remote houses.'

'Thanks Trevor,'' said Priscilla warmly. 'I look forward to seeing you again.'

As Trevor landed, the darkness now covered the escarpment making it look even more foreboding. Stepping down from the helicopter, Priscilla commented on how different it all looked to when they were last there, only months ago.

'Maybe it's because it's still the wet season; things change from wet to dry season here remarkably,' replied Dee trying to sound confident as the helicopter disappeared into the gloom.

It took them a while to find the cave they had sheltered in on their last expedition and thankfully located it just as the storm hit. The rain cascaded and howling winds blanketed the area as they huddled in the shelter provided by the overhanging rock ledge.

There were no signs of their last visit and no footprints of recent inhabitants. For several hours the deluge continued and they decided to camp the night under the ledge; it was warm and dry and too late to go searching – west of their position – for the entrance down to the caves they'd found on their original expedition with Simon.

Sleep came eventually as the storm continued unabated, only easing towards morning as Dee made a small fire, boiled the Billy for some tea and a breakfast of fruit bars. Streaks of the sun's rays heralded the new day but they knew that by midday it would be hot and humid. Unlike their last visit, water lay everywhere in pools and small streams ran over bare rock before disappearing into chasms that ran directly down into hidden areas, like the one they had stumbled upon on the first trip. Dee and Priscilla calculated their entrance to the hidden valley must only be under a kilometre west from their position or slightly more, and set off skirting rocky outcrops and deep fissures in the rocks that would trap any individual or animal should they stumble into them.

By mid-morning they were rather alarmed at not being able to recognise any point or landscape they had previously seen. Every hundred metres they would go round in a wide circle looking for *anything* that looked like the entrance that they had existed in from months before. By midday they were shattered. The packs were heavy and the air humid. They sat beneath a crag, baffled at their inability to locate the entrance to the amphitheatre that they *knew* existed nearby. Heavy threatening clouds began to form again north of their position. Dee had been looking at the area south of their position when he jumped to his feet.

'I think I see it! Now I remember! We came out behind a rather prominent rock face. I think that is it behind the one to our left; we've passed it twice!' Dee exclaimed.

Priscilla staggered to her feet and suddenly feeling motivated, walked briskly towards the outcrop. Skirting around the base they grinned at each other, for there, sitting below was the track leading directly down into the area they had so painfully left months before.

They wound their way down; vegetation had grown during the wet season and several pieces of the steep shelf had fallen away to the depths below. On the descent, sweat trickled down their faces and bodies from the oppressive humidity which increased with each step as they laboured downwards. They passed the two main caves and rested in the one that contained the burial chambers, marvelling at the generations of Stone People who lay before them. When they reached the spot where Priscilla had broken her ankle, they wound the ropes they'd been carrying around several sturdy shrubs and Dee, with both backpacks, slowly made two trips across the now even more dangerous area before helping Priscilla over. When they were at the bottom, they acknowledged *why* this area would never be seen from the air because from above, it would simply appear as a dark hole. It was possibly several hundred metres to the top, and nature had provided for an opening less than half the area of the bottom.

When they'd located their old camp site, they dropped the packs, and like two enthusiastic teenagers, rushed around inspecting but were disappointed that there were no signs of the Stone People. They appreciated that the wet season would have wiped out all tracks including their own and in the dry caves, only animal prints were evident. Just as they stepped inside the cave where the badly injured girl had been found, the roar of a fast- approaching storm saw them scamper for the backpacks and drag them into the cave. The small stream that ran through the cave was raging as they climbed to higher ground, then prepared a small fire. Their exploration would have to wait until the next day.

FIFTEEN

During the long night Dee kept the small fire burning; its flames casting a ghostly light that danced around the cave walls. The river raged and thunder crashed outside with lightning lighting up the area with its blinding flashes.

As daylight began to appear, they heard a loud groaning, then thunderous rumbling. Running to the cave mouth they froze in horror as the ledge they had so carefully climbed down was crashing below. Tons of rock cascaded and no sooner had it hit the bottom when the rain eased and an eerie silence descended. Dee and Priscilla looked at each other, devastated and in shock.

'Don't worry; we still have the goat track we came in on. We'll just have to go out that way,' said Dee as he comforted the distraught Priscilla.

In shock, Priscilla replied, 'No phone in here so you're right Dee; we'll explore today, taking only sufficient food and water and the small day-pack and head back the way Simon came in. Not looking forward to it but we've no choice.'

'Obviously the Stone People haven't been here since the dry and now they've been cut off as well, but I'm sure they know of other routes in and out. The escarpment runs for hundreds of kilometres so I guess they only come here for burials or when someone is about to die,' replied Dee with a dry mouth.

The prospect of exiting the area had suddenly lost its shine. They scoured the area but were unable to find any exit apart from the one they came in on. There were no fresh signs of the Stone People and ultimately had to admit that the place only had significance as a burial chamber; a place they came to die and be with their ancestors. Using binoculars to inspect the area on the opposite side of the cave they'd sheltered in, Dee gasped and cried out, 'Look! The caves! They're also gone. When the ledge crumbled last night, the entrances collapsed and now they're sealed under tons of rock!'

'Unbelievable!' cried a fraught Priscilla. 'Gone forever; even to the remaining Stone People, buried for all time.'

'Absolutely,' Dee replied sighing. 'The only proof that they ever existed are our photos and as we don't intend to use them, the existence of centuries of a pygmy race is now lost forever.'

'Why don't we leave all our records to the next generation? When George and his generation are gone, and us two my love, Australia might be ready for such knowledge but I doubt if by that time, any of the Stone People will have survived,' suggested Priscilla frowning.

Despite their ongoing search, they could not find any other route other than the exit they knew of that would take them out of the amphitheatre. The landslide had diminished a substantial part of the region and despite their best efforts, they were hemmed in. That evening, they huddled round the campfire feeling deflated and somewhat anxious. Little did they know that no other living person on earth knew where they were.

Upon leaving his two passengers, Trevor Adams had tracked north for some time trying to outdistance the storm. He had never encountered one with such a wide front and from his observations, knew it was more intense than any he had confronted during his few short years flying in Arnhem Land. He became alarmed and decided to turn back and travel south along the fringe of the escarpment and if necessary, land and sit the storm out. He tracked south, trying to raise Darwin but without success and then his instruments began to malfunction due to the electrical storm that now enveloped him. For the first time in his life, Trevor was afraid. Without instruments he became disorientated and flew lower to try and locate a safe landing area; he knew that to fly on was foolhardy and dangerous.

With visibility now almost zero, he did not see the towering rock outcrop. His machine ploughed into it, disintegrating into hundreds of pieces killing him instantly. A mayday was sent out when hours later he was reported missing and the major search that followed unfortunately found no trace. Trevor and his helicopter remained a mystery. He was presumed killed and that he had somehow crashed during the storm. The main search took place well away from the location of the crash site. Dropping off his clients and then heading further south had taken Trevor well off his usual flight path.

No one assumed he had any passengers onboard. George's son had picked up the vehicle Dee and Priscilla left at the airport and they and others assumed that they had caught a flight to Darwin and on to Sydney, as they had told no one else other than Trevor of their plans to enter the Escarpment Country again. If Dee and Priscilla had been aware of these tragic events, their mindset would have been a lot different. They believed that if they did not show up or call Trevor, he would obviously raise the alarm and one of the first people he would notify would be Simon Black.

And so it was that the following morning, oblivious of the tragic helicopter crash and demise of the pilot, Dee and Priscilla set off with light packs down the narrow path between sheer walls on either side. Their goal was to make it out before evening, despite the long day ahead of them. Even their previous experience did not make it any easier and they agreed it was far worse than they remembered. After three hours they stopped and looked at each other; fear and resignation weighed heavily as they saw what lay before them; the track was blocked by boulders making passage impossible. Collapsing to their knees they inhaled deeply, knowing they were trapped. They needed rescuing and only Simon would know their location.

Neither spoke as they about-turned and headed back to the main area; at least they had provisions – if they were careful – to last two weeks.

By the time they broke into the hidden canyon that was now to be their home until rescue, Dee and Priscilla slumped to the ground with stress and exhaustion. They curled up around the fire and let the darkness embrace them.

Dee slept badly and when he woke up, saw Priscilla sitting with her head in her hands. Hearing his movement, she looked up at him and spoke for the first time in tones of defeat.

'Dee, I'm so sorry I insisted on coming back again; I should have known better. History is a great teacher and this is not called Debil Debil country for nothing; every expedition here in the past has ended in tragedy or near tragedy.'

'My darling Priscilla this was my choice too. To be honest, my life had been crap anyhow until I met you again that day in Sydney. I'm one big fake. Depression has always haunted me and you might have thought that I was the life and soul of the party but it was a front. If I had my choices again, without a blink of an eyelid I would have chosen the same course just to be with you and if we die here, then I regard it as a privilege to have married you and spent such quality time with you, so no more bad thoughts, think positive, miracles happen and Trevor will raise the alarm. If he hears nothing from us and Simon is smart, he will know we're here,' answered Dee standing up.

Priscilla wept and stood up to walk over to Dee. They embraced and kissed each other with such passion like the fire blazing near them.

They set off again to investigate the perimeter of the hidden canyon, trying to locate any way up the sheer walls to freedom above but all avenues explored resulted in a dead end. Even the ropes they had had lay buried beneath tons of rock. With each trip away from the campsite, they collected armfuls of precious firewood; all the vegetation was small and didn't last long so they only kept a small fire going and only used it for cooking when necessary. Laying all the provisions out, they calculated that, if from now on they only ate two light meals a day, surprisingly, three weeks remained before the food would run out. They had identified a small community of rock wallaby living under the vegetation in several locations so they tried to think of a way to kill these when, and if, needed.

Much to her surprise, after Dee's confession, Priscilla decided to make the most of the time they had. If all else failed, she had to accept her fate whatever it might be. Dee used several small stems of various shrubs to try and fashion a bow. For two days he tried without success, until one spindly-looking plant proved successful enough to fire a small arrow he'd fashioned from the same tree. For string he used some of the webbing, and for the arrowhead, they fashioned one of the knives that they carried and bound it with the same canvas string that Priscilla had fashioned for the bow string; again, this small achievement gave them strength as they desperately clung to the belief, that in a few days, Trevor would raise the alarm.

Priscilla then began to worry about how she had never been one for making friends with her neighbours and now regretted it. She was often away and felt isolated in that no one would notice or care about her absence, perhaps for years! Because of all her travelling, she'd arranged for rates to be paid via her bank and it would take years before anyone became alarmed. *Her electricity power had been paid for by card in advance and once that ran out, who would care? Who would know?*

Priscilla never mentioned her thoughts on all this to Dee but she did worry that their fate was in the hands of one individual and in hindsight, cursed herself for being so foolish. Her only other thought and it was a long shot, was if the little people returned and noticed the campfire below, but on reflection, she knew that if this did occur, they had no way of rescuing them.

Days dragged by and Dee shot his first wallaby. They cooked the meat slowly and were surprised at how tasty it was. It lasted them two days, leaving it like the Aboriginals to slowly cook in the coals whilst breaking off what they needed. This small effort raised their spirits as well as the river in the rear of the cave which had subsided and allowed them to swim and splash. The water was warm and therapeutic.

Two weeks passed and Dee found his razor so blunt he gave up shaving; Priscilla teased him that he was beginning to look like a caveman. They vigilantly washed their clothes regularly and tried to maintain dress standards as high as possible; it gave them a psychological lift to change into fresh clothes after a good frolic in the warm cave stream. Time seemed to drag and they grew alarmed as to why no one had come to rescue them. One evening, while sitting around the campfire, a cold chill came over Priscilla and she shivered.

'Dee, I've just had the most shocking thought; what if something happened to Trevor, what if he had an accident in Darwin or he crashed or something terrible!' she said trembling, her voice rising hysterically. She looked at Dee plaintively, seeking reassurance.

'Priscilla my love, if that *did* happen and the chances are remote; then we *are* sitting in our tomb. I'm beginning to face the reality that even if he did take two weeks before he raised the alarm, Simon would have long been up above glassing below for any signs of us being here. Those thoughts went through my head several days ago to be honest,' replied Dee wistfully. That night, they slept entwined in each other's arms. A new sense of defeatism invaded them and the possible inevitable slow demise of starvation became a stark reality. If, for some reason unknown, Trevor didn't manage to raise the alarm; then they both knew that only weeks remained of their lives.

They tried, as far as possible, to save the few remaining tins of food when the tea and sugar ran out. Dee spent most days hunting but the dwindling numbers of wallaby became an issue. They had taken to hanging the carcasses in the cooler part of the cave and stretching the meat supply for as many days as possible before they became putrid.

Another two weeks passed. They were resigned to the fact that no rescue was forthcoming. It was beyond all belief; a simple return journey to seek out contact with the Stone People was now going to cost them their lives. Oddly, they accepted their fate and cherished each day as it came and went, settling into a routine and desperately trying to keep positive. They chatted to each other, desperately ignoring their impending fate.

SIXTEEN

Awakening from a troubled sleep, Dee carefully removed Priscilla's arm from over his shoulder and rose to place some kindling on the smouldering fire. Looking down at her, he felt such strong love for her even though they now looked dishevelled and gaunt. Dee knew deep in his heart that they were weak and he had even noticed Priscilla becoming disorientated; her mind beginning to crack under the strain of knowing the inevitable.

Drinking a long draft of water to try and ease the constant hunger and stomach cramp pains that now plagued them; he started his morning walk to the back of the cave to replenish the camp water supply. Although the distance was only a short way, it took him thirty minutes. The now, almost idle stream, ran into a cavern and here a pool of clear water lay. Filling the two canteens, Dee sat to rest on a small ledge adjacent to the pool, staring into the water. His heart skipped a beat, as rising majestically from the pool like a vision, was a male from the Stone People they had met before! He hardly made a ripple and then the rest of his group followed, including the young girl Priscilla had so carefully attended to!

Dee beamed at them and they chatted to him in a dialect he did not understand. He then cursed himself for not thinking about exploring beneath where the stream flowed. *Why had he been so stupid?*

Following the little group with incredible lightness in his step, they approached a slumbering Priscilla who, upon waking, saw in the hazy mist of her mind the Stone People standing before her! The young girl knelt and offered Priscilla some bush fruit that she had in a small, woven pouch.

Gulping down the fruit, Priscilla started to sob uncontrollably, blubbering to Dee, 'How did they get in here?'

Dee explained how they had just suddenly appeared from beneath the river and as Priscilla was helped up by her saviours, shaking and incredibly weak with hunger, she swooned and had to be sat down again by her new carers who seemed extremely concerned as to her welfare.

Two of the stone men disappeared as the remainder fed Dee and Priscilla with the balance of the fruit they carried. That little bit of sustenance, together with renewed optimism, gave Dee and Priscilla strength that beyond all expectation, they might actually survive.

The two men who had left earlier returned with a wallaby and threw it on the fire; skin, guts and all. A wonderful aroma of cooking meat filled the cave as the band of Stone People squatted on their haunches, chatting away, completely at ease with Priscilla and Dee. No doubt their original meeting had taught them that no harm would come from them and that they had nursed a member of their group back to health.

Priscilla noticed the wound had healed well and although there was a noticeable scar and she did still limp slightly, much to Priscilla's delight, she noticed a small bump which indicated she was probably pregnant!

During that night, poor Priscilla suffered stomach cramps and diaorrhea. Her body was weaker than ever and she was incoherent. Dee tended to her during the night and found himself struggling as he did not have the physical strength to lift her.

On one of their many trips to the toilet area they'd constructed, they were shocked into silence and stared at each other in utter defeat; the Stone People had moved on. Dee stumbled to the cave and to his utter disappointment tracked them into the water as silently as they had arrived, they had disappeared.

Priscilla and Dee knew that these nomads had no idea of the dire circumstances they had found them in because in their society, those unable to keep up or fell ill were simply left behind and the rest would continue with the day-to-day life of survival.

The realisation of their departure resulted in Priscilla becoming even more despondent and her speech began to deteriorate. Dee then fully accepted that it was up to him to try and get them out of their tomb. Sorting through the few possessions they still had, he filled a small day-pack with a few items of clothing. Knowing he had to help Priscilla was enough to contend with but he picked up his bow and sole arrow, and managed to get Priscilla to her feet and headed into the cave.

Arriving at the pool, Dee sat her gently on the sand. It was almost semi-darkness and it took some time for his eyes to adjust from the external sunlight. With the day-pack in his hand, he instructed Priscilla to wait whilst he checked out the exit and ducked under the cover and into the water. To his surprise, the exit was only about one metre and Dee knew that another few weeks into the dry season and the entrance would be exposed, coming out the other side of a chamber. Daylight, streaming from a small opening above, showed a track leading to what he thought would be south.

Returning to Priscilla, Dee helped her under the rock shelf into the chamber and with his bow and pack, slowly wound their way along the edge of the river for a few hundred metres before sitting on the sand to rest; breathing slowly and heavily. Dee intended to follow the clear, fresh footprints of the Stone People, knowing that eventually they would break into more open country. On several occasions they had problems with picking the path around boulders and often Dee went ahead whilst Priscilla rested. Despite many obstacles, they were determined to continue as far as possible before darkness.

On one of the stops, they chewed the last of the wallaby left by the Stone People, easing the growing hunger but unfortunately the result made Priscilla sick again; her stomach was simply rejecting food. During the day they did not speak. Preserving energy was crucial. Dee knew that the next forty-eight hours were critical. If they failed to break out into open country and find food they would die. They hollowed an incline in the sand near a prominent overhanging ledge and Dee anticipated that there would be no late storm as the land above would empty into the chamber, causing the river to rise rapidly, thereby trapping them. A cold sweat broke out at the prospect.

With no wood for a fire they really felt the cold. Dee pulled Priscilla to her feet, even though she was shaking uncontrollably, and got her to walk in circles; he stamping his feet while roughly massaging Priscilla to keep her circulation going and warm her as best as he could; given the circumstances. As soon as the first rays of sunshine hit the walls far above, Dee decided to move on but with Priscilla's walk now only a shuffle, he had no idea how long it was going to take them. All he knew was that time was running out and if they did not get out of the labyrinth that day, they would die.

To Dee's astonishment the river became wider and deeper. Several landslides had, over time, now made it even more gruelling to navigate and several times Dee had to carry Priscilla around colossal, obtrusive boulders. He noted trees that had crashed from above and in doing so, lost the tracks of the Stone People. *Did they know of another track to the top?* he wondered. *Had he missed it and if so, was there ever going to be a way out if he continued further.*

Dee stopped at around midday, ready to drop. He made a fire with some of the broken branches and stared at the flames which were comforting. Priscilla sat gazing vacantly. Dee saw the blank expression on her face and felt a terrible sense of wretchedness and grief. He had always been a loner and although he had had a few relationships, none had been more than convenience. He now knew that in Priscilla, he had found his soul mate; his first true love and now he was going to have to watch her die slowly and in agony. Engrossed in their own deep thoughts, they sat by a pool of water. Dee then got up very, very slowly. He could not believe what he had just seen; a silver barramundi cruised past him obviously trapped in the pool. Fitting his arrow to the bow, and with the last of his strength, Dee let the arrow go and hit the fish in the middle of its back. Splashing and yelling like a banshee, Dee hit the water grabbing the fish and immediately cut off thin strips as he and Priscilla tore into the flesh like people possessed.

He placed several bite-sized chunks onto sticks and still eating the raw fish, slowly cooked the remainder of the food. The cooked fish would last a few days with the water; all being well, these two basic needs would keep them alive for a few more days. Unfortunately it caused stomach cramps again for Priscilla so Dee decided to stay where they were until she was feeling stronger. To his surprise and utter delight, Priscilla kept the fresh fish down and as the pains eased during the night, he gently fed her on the cooked fish. It then dawned on Dee that the stomach cramps had been caused by the fruit-like food the Stone People had given them. Obviously their digestive system had adapted to certain foods whereas his and Priscilla's had rejected it. Just the thought of this offered Dee optimism knowing that the river was a source of healthy fish and protein. Dee wandered up the river further and returned carrying a fresh-water crocodile. He skinned and cooked the white pork-like meat, rather pleased with himself at his recently discovered ability to provide off the land for them.

With a constant supply of protein, Priscilla's health began to improve. They had remained at the site for three days and during this time, Dee had even washed the remnants of their now truly scruffy clothes. They washed nude in the warm water. He was startled and shocked at their appearance; almost skeletal.

It was then that Dee told Priscilla that they *would* survive and that no matter what, they would adapt to the terrain and climate. As Priscilla began to improve, they decided it would be best to stay with the river during the dry season and then, when the wet season commenced, to try again to find a way out. They knew they were totally lost. The phone battery had long since gone flat in the valley where they had initially been trapped and Dee had left it with the other bags that were too heavy to carry. They had to adopt the lifestyle of the Stone People; travel light and live off the land.

Catching that first fish had changed Dee's mindset and he now made another arrow, along with fashioning a spear which he practised throwing. His new attitude was contagious and as Priscilla regained her strength, she went in search of bush food; wanting to participate in their survival. She successfully found some lilies in one of the caverns and the roots were refreshing and filling; each success strengthening them.

With no further Stone People tracks, it was obvious that the group had left their path some time ago. For another week they followed the ever-widening ravine south, working out the direction by the sunrise each day. There was plenty of fish and their physical and mental outlook improved enormously.

One evening, while wading in a pool hunting for fish, Dee gave a yell as he pointed south to an opening in the cliff face some distance away. Running like mad men, they made the distance in minutes, crying and falling into each other's arms. To their right heading west was *open country*, rough and sparse with small shrubs but open country; they had actually managed to break free!

Back at their camp, Priscilla and Dee were jubilant and verging on hysteria. That night they discussed seriously their chances of survival and admitted that they had a good chance if and only if, they agreed that commonsense prevailed.

'Firstly Priscilla my love, apart from us looking like absolute shit, we are gradually adapting and learning daily how to survive in this environment. But if we leave water in the dry season and head west to God knows where, we won't stand a chance; we'll die of thirst and starvation. Here, on the river, we have two vital essentials; water and food. I feel strongly that we should remain here until the wet is under way,' said Dee, now smiling as he looked at Priscilla.

'Yes, you're right; *we must think every move*. Having made it to this point, let's not jeopardise matters. The river is getting smaller so we must be getting near the head waters. As bad as it sounds, behind us are pools of fish, freshwater crocs and in the wider lagoons, water lilies, along with the turtles of which all have served us well,' replied Priscilla now with confidence.

'In other words my darling, "we" are now living an Indigenous life! And yes, what you say is true; we'd be mad to leave here now even with our canteens. In two days the cooked meat will be off and the water will run out, we have no choice but to stay here,' responded Dee with some authority. Having been provided with food from the river, he was without doubt that Priscilla was right.

SEVENTEEN

For four months Priscilla and Dee hunted and mastered their survival skills across the area deep inside the escarpment. There was plenty of fish in the bigger pools and they became adept at spearing them; competing with each other as hunter-gatherers. They failed to gain weight but their fitness surpassed anything either had known before in their previous easy lifestyle.

The last of the clothes were now rags so they simply wore skirts from the remnants. Lean, tanned and fit, their lovemaking began again but this time with more passion and fire than ever before. They were lost in their own world and content without the possessions that white civilisation seems to demand and require. Yes, they were waiting for the wet season but having survived all that they had experienced, everything else was irrelevant.

As the dry continued, several of the minor waterholes dried up, making their hunt for food more challenging. Luckily, Dee managed to hunt a few wallabies but the pressure was constant; a daily test of their skills but one that they strangely enjoyed.

They did wonder how this experience would impact their lives if and when they returned to civilisation.

Priscilla told Dee that she honestly felt she might *never* be able to settle in Sydney and that if he agreed to sell the house and buy a yacht, why couldn't they just sail to isolated and unexplored islands? Enthusiastically Dee did agree. The prospect of going home and trying to lead a normal life again was nigh impossible after the dramatic change in their life experiences. Their lives, as they once knew them, had changed forever.

And so the days moved into weeks and the imminent wet season never entered the long conversations they shared. Each day they explored, experimented with new hunting techniques and new bush foods. Their daily routine was entwined in a new world; their previous lives surreal and seemingly so long ago. A mob of wild ducks landed near the camp one day and the two hunters gently picked up their spears and crawled close to the unsuspecting birds. Rising slowly to their feet, they hurled the spears with all their might, killing two instantly. Wild yelps of delight vibrated across the land as they ran shrieking into the water to retrieve the hapless birds. Returning to the campfire they threw the two dead ducks onto the coals, completely forgetting the usual custom of cleaning and plucking! They had well and truly adapted to the wilderness and in a short six months. They tore drumsticks off the ducks, oblivious that they had transitioned to those who have lived that lifestyle for centuries. They stuffed themselves and did not save any for later; *living in the moment*, happy, content and wanting nothing more than a full belly and each other.

Two months later, signs of the wet season appeared; dark clouds began to roll in and distant thunder rattled across the escarpment. One night, as they chatted about the day's events, the Stone People appeared again as if from nowhere! They promptly sat around the fire as if they'd never left all those months before. Priscilla was overjoyed to see her friend now carrying a baby, only a few weeks old. Priscilla made a gesture that she would like to hold the baby and the young girl got up, walked around the fire and placed the baby into Priscilla's arms. Priscilla was in her element. Regretting not having had a child, Priscilla often voiced her sadness at not meeting Dee when she was still capable of bearing a child; but now she felt like this tiny infant was part of her family and a look of a maternal grandmother came over Priscilla as the infant fastened on to her nipple, squirming contentedly in her arms.

For two days their guests stayed in camp joining them on their hunting forays. Dee especially enjoyed the new skills he picked up from his companions whilst Priscilla stayed in camp; infatuated with the baby and caring for it while its mother left camp with the women to look for food. On the third morning, the group once again made ready for departure but this time Dee and Priscilla simply picked up their spears and few possessions and wandered off with the Stone People. They had been accepted as part of the tribe and trusted members.

That first day wandering along with one of the most stone-age people left on the planet, was one of total freedom and happiness for Priscilla and Dee. Priscilla carried the infant; beaming with pride that here, she had a family and was part of people's lives; she was consumed with love for her tiny responsibility. They had to learn to slow down to the snail pace of the little group who had no time constraints or schedule; they merely enjoyed the land from which they were always looking for a food source. Daily sustenance in the way of protein was their priority, especially with two more mouths to feed.

During those first few days, Dee and Priscilla soon learned that their hunting ability, although reasonable, paled into insignificance when compared to their hosts. Dee was a quick learner and eager and in the first week, gained enormous respect from his co-hunters; in addition, albeit ever so slowly, they began to learn the dialect of the group. Completely at ease now with the contentment of living in a group and unaware of their exact location, Dee and Priscilla forgot about the plans to head west in the wet season and succumbed to living with the abundance provided by the wet season with bush fruits and fish teaming in the swollen rivers. Although unsure of their location, they assumed that they had travelled well south of the location where they were originally trapped. It now seemed a lifetime ago. Dee and Priscilla felt safe and accepted, and neither wanted to take a chance and leave the group, thereby risking starvation again. Priscilla's infatuation with the baby was another important factor in wanting to remain with the group. She felt needed, and loved their simple, uncomplicated life. Yes, it was harsh and unrelenting but she had survived and adapted; she felt that "she had come home". Dee was happy and felt he belonged but more pertinently, his love for Priscilla, since their survival, burned even brighter than ever and to see her so happy was his only wish. Time now stood still for these two people, living as their ancestors must have done centuries before; the simple life of a hunter-gatherer.

****

Two years passed. Priscilla's garden in Sydney became overgrown so the next door neighbour cleaned up the yard. He was aware of her nomadic lifestyle and considered that on her return she would gladly reimburse him for the costs. The helicopter accident disappeared into history, their friends thought no more about it as they had all been missing for many years. Simon Black never thought of Dee and Priscilla as his life as a guide continued but old George and Mary often looked west to the escarpment. Of all their friends, George felt that Priscilla had returned and that she must be okay. He wasn't surprised they hadn't come back to see him – he simply got on with his life – it was the Aboriginal way.

Priscilla's day was taken up rummaging for food with her young, adopted child following her everywhere. Its mother was heavily pregnant for the second time. From a distance, apart from size, Dee and Priscilla, with their skin baked brown and naked except for the hair belt they wore; looked like local inhabitants. One distinction was Dee's flowing beard and Priscilla's long hair that hung to her waist.

The thought of leaving may never have surfaced but when one of the elder women found it hard to keep up and contribute to the group, the rest of the group, when passing another burial cave, simply left her sitting at the entrance. Her time had come and she alone had made her choice to find a spare shelf in the cave and remain there to die with her ancestors.

Priscilla was upset and for the first time an argument took place until Dee intervened; calming Priscilla down and explaining how they *had* to abide by the rules of the Stone People. Necessity meant that their long-held traditions had to be respected in order to survive and a "useless" person to feed was a burden on the rest.

That evening, Priscilla was still extremely distressed at leaving a human to die and for the first time discussed with Dee that it might be the time for them to leave; two older men in the group had made plans to also enter the afterlife which would only leave an unsustainable group left. Now fluent in their language, Priscilla pleaded with her young friend to accompany them back to civilisation but her reaction was immediate; the thought of going out of the escarpment terrified her and she told Priscilla that the "big people" would kill and eat her. Priscilla gave up trying to persuade her knowing it would be a waste of time and cause more friction. She had already upset things in her arguing for the old woman's life.

That same day, during the evening, Dee confided in Priscilla that he too thought it was time for them to leave;

they were confident of their skills and he was now concerned for their safety. The remaining men became suspicious of them; obviously afraid that Priscilla would leave with the child she loved so much. They feared she would kidnap her.

Dee did his best to explain to the remaining members that they would leave and head back to their own country; the news seemed to pacify them and they pointed east to the coast as the better way out.

And so, without any fanfare, Dee and Priscilla picked up the few belongings and with heavy hearts, walked off into the bush, picking their way into the unknown. Priscilla never looked back. Tears poured down her cheeks because she knew they would never see this unique group of people again, but in her heart she knew it was time to go home.

No longer afraid of their surroundings they walked until darkness before finding a spot to camp for the evening. Dee made the fire and they tried to settle for the night. In times past, they would have slept lightly; frightened of the wild environment but now they were confident and comfortable and slept well. Used to the slow progress of the group they had lived with for several years, they too ambled slowly along, guided by the rising sun each morning, heading northeast from the Escarpment Country. Food was easy to come by and Dee, with Priscilla's help, killed a pig and enjoyed a meal of roast pork. Buffalo and wild cattle were sighted but they chose not to attempt those beasts with their primitive weapons.

Priscilla and Dee had no idea of the sight they presented

until about a week into their journey. A rough bush track appeared, and Dee had an idea that this was one he had travelled on with Simon and so they followed its easterly direction. By midmorning they came across a camp fire, where some Aboriginal children and three adults were sitting around the fire chatting loudly as well as a vehicle nearby. On seeing the wild-looking couple, mayhem broke out with women and children screaming as they tried to cram themselves into the already overloaded vehicle. One of the men started the vehicle and dropped the clutch, leaving several of them running and screaming down the road in pursuit to disappear from view in the thick bush; the screams of fear still resounding across the landscape.

Dee and Priscilla looked at each other in shock at what they had just witnessed and then broke into uncontrollable fits of laughter. Looking wild and emaciated and clutching a handful of spears, they must have looked like the absolute worst to the group of Aboriginals. The old stories and legends of the Debil Debil country just became a reality for the terrified Aboriginals. Dee was grateful that none of them had firearms but now at least he knew they had struck the Gove to Numbulwar track and that it would lead them to Simon Black's camp.

Years of living rough and walking long distances daily now kicked in as they strode along with a new sense of purpose, knowing that within at least a day's walk, Simon's camp would provide baths and clean clothes, although having not worn shoes or clothes for so long might create a problem.

EIGHTEEN

Simon and two guests sat around the camp fire celebrating a successful day. His clients had shot a magnificent trophy bull and were enjoying a glass of wine as they relived the day's events.

Simon heard a vehicle approaching and cocked his ears. Although it was coming fast, it was not unusual because during the dry, several carloads of Indigenous people made the journey and he knew they would stop and ask for fuel and food. This was a regular occurrence and Simon knew that to refuse giving fuel and food meant stranded, starving children; so he steeled himself for the request.

He soon established; however, that something was not right. The vehicle was overcrowded with at least thirteen adults and children screaming past the occupants and hysterically pointing backwards behind them. Through the window, they yelled out to Simon and his guests, 'Debil Debil coming!' The vehicle hit the stream south of his camp and water sprayed in the air as it disappeared in a massive shower of water and steam, leaving Simon and his two guests staring in amazement.

'Let's get into the car and go and see what exactly is "coming" on the track that caused such a reaction,' said Simon to his guests as he collected his thoughts.

Sandra and Keith Williams took no convincing as they were just as curious as Simon to discover what the terrified carload had seen.

Simon had only driven for about five minutes when to his absolute astonishment, he saw two bedraggled-looking figures coming towards him down the road. The figures were waving madly at them; his two guests sat rigid.

'Holy shit! What is this?' shrieked Sandra Williams. 'Never knew you had wild bush people here goddamn.'

Simon pulled up and peering at the two odd-looking figures, recognised Dee.

'Dee, is that *really* you?' he asked breathlessly.

Dee, having not conversed with another English-speaking person apart from Priscilla, replied, 'Yes Simon, it's me and this is Priscilla! We've sort of been lost for a few years.'

Priscilla's emotions took over and she stood crying uncontrollably, while Simon jumped out and hurriedly opened the rear door to help them into the back of the vehicle.

'Grab the spears! They're history – don't leave them here!' cried Keith Williams excitedly.

'Keith you're amazing; leave the fucking spears, get them later! Can't you see we have two humans here in deep shit!' yelled Sandra above the mayhem.

'Let's get you back and cleaned up, then we'll get the full story, and I guess you certainly have one to tell,' interrupted Simon shaking his head in utter disbelief.

'Thanks,' muttered an emotional Dee. His voice was raspy.

It then hit Dee and Priscilla that they had survived. They had cheated death *twice* in the Escarpment Country. It was finally over.

It also only hit them after they arrived back at camp that they were actually naked apart from their waistbands! It had never occurred to them that such a thing was unacceptable but now they were back in "civilisation". Sandra Williams owned a beauty salon in Texas and as soon as Dee and Priscilla stepped out of the vehicle, it became her destiny in life to get them showered and spruced up. Simon produced a set of hair clippers and scissors and while her two "clients" ate and drank some strong coffee, Sandra clipped away and cut years of matted, dirty hair, firstly from Priscilla. Sandra had so many clothes and insisted that Priscilla wear one of the many safari outfits she had brought with her.

Simon suggested that after showering and dressing, they should have some dinner and then hit the sack. They all needed a decent night's sleep before sitting down to breakfast and hearing what he knew, would be a remarkable story.

It was well after dark when Sandra finally gave her nod of approval. Her husband had happily offered Dee some of his clothing. He dare not behave otherwise; not a good idea to overrule his wife's wishes as Sandra Williams had a mission to restore two people who had survived years in the wilderness, back to civility.

On completion of the major clean-up, sitting around the camp fire after a meal and some wine, exhaustion wrapped itself around Dee and Priscilla and they wearily retreated to a soft bed for the first time in several years. Within minutes, they were asleep.

It was mid-morning before they eventually left the bliss of comfort. They were well rested and went to join the others in the main safari kitchen to enjoy toast and coffee. Dee noticed that Sandra and Keith were extremely anxious to hear their story as they only had two days left and had shot their quota; they were quite happy to forego a day's fishing to hear their incredible tale.

'Before I begin, you *must* promise that what I say will stay within these walls,' announced Dee sipping his coffee.

'Hell man, why, this story can make you rich! It'll go all over the world; *Couple survive in wild country for five years!'* blurted Keith.

'No, when you hear the full story, I sincerely believe you'll understand,' explained Dee quietly.

'Yes Dee, we promise; *don't we Keith,'* replied Sandra giving her husband a cold stare.

Keith nodded and Dee slowly began from the beginning, filling in the last five years of their lives. Priscilla sat in silence whilst the other three sat enthralled at the story that unfolded.

When Dee finished, it was way past lunchtime.

'Now I remember the chopper crash! That must have been your chopper and pilot; the timing works in, I forgot about it. No wonder he was never found; to drop you off would have taken him well off course,' Simon informed them.

The news, although expected, shattered Dee and Priscilla. Somehow they felt responsible for Trevor's death as he had been doing them a favour. Simon tried to comfort them by saying that in reality, from what he remembered, the storm had been a once-in-a-hundred-year event and could have happened at any time. He was certain that that is what caused the landslides in the Escarpment Country; the lowlands were inundated and his camp had been under water for weeks, even though it sat seventy feet above the Walker River.

Although the others were elated at their survival, the reality of what had happened began to sink in. As they retreated to bed after lunch, Priscilla stood before the mirror and commented, 'Dee, how on earth can you love this body? I'm a wrinkled up old woman! Look at my saggy tits and my vagina has more hair now than my head since Sandra bobbed it all off!'

Laughing, Dee replied, 'My darling girl, I'm not so great myself. Actually, look a bit of a moron with the crew cut I got! I'm aware this is going to be a hard trip back for us but the reality is we have no choice, so chin up, we have each other and my God, we satisfied ourselves about the Stone People, that's for sure.'

Turning to face him, Priscilla continued, mulling things over and thinking about the future, 'Dee, another problem, our wallets. We left them back in the cavern we got trapped in, so until we get back home, we've no money.'

'No problem. Simon'll pay our airfares home to Sydney and our cards will all have expired anyhow,' answered Dee reassuringly.

Priscilla seemed to be satisfied with the answer and with

a deep sigh, dozed off peacefully but Dee knew the turmoil they would face after five years of living in a stone-age society. Readjusting to the complicated modern world would prove interesting to say the least.

Over dinner that evening, Simon had already figured out the problems they faced and had arranged a flight the following day to Darwin, then a connecting flight home. He handed them a few hundred dollars for which Priscilla thanked him and she and Dee promised to transfer funds as soon as they arrived Sydney. Not surprisingly, Dee and Priscilla didn't sleep well that night as the prospect of flying now appeared an immense obstacle and they were dreading it.

Simon waved a fond farewell to his two friends and the last of his clients for that season; he would return to camp and lock up until the following season. He had his vehicle packed for the drive into Darwin and was ruminating over the last few days' events. How they had survived was beyond comprehension but they had. They had adapted and come out alive. Unfortunately, Simon knew that their story would never be told. The Aboriginals would tell their frightening tale but no one would believe it and like all good stories, would eventually fade away.

With no baggage to collect, Priscilla and Dee caught a taxi around to the Domestic Terminal, saying their goodbyes to Sandra and Keith who had to wait for a number of pieces of luggage to then transfer to the International Terminal. Arriving at the front counter, Dee and Priscilla requested their tickets, a smiling staff member requested ID in the form of a licence or passport. Dee explained they had lost everything in Arnhem Land and had neither.

'I am sorry sir, we have to have ID,' harped the attendant, now puffed up with authority.

'*I* am sorry but did you not hear me? We lost our luggage in Arnhem Land and have no documents at all,' explained Dee patiently, knowing he would get nowhere with this particular attendant.

Priscilla stepped forward, 'We can argue all day and waste each other's time; please get your senior in charge, now. *Please*, the aircraft is loading.'

Throwing her head in the air, the officious one went out the back and returned with an older man. When Priscilla explained the circumstances; he simply waved them through, much to the disgust of the "officious one".

The encounter was just another reminder of the kind of life they were returning to. Gone was the simplistic and carefree life in the bush; they now had to accept and embrace the regimentation of modern society and the officials who thrived in the nanny state they had created. On board the plane, they sat together on the outside; an executive-looking woman was already seated in the window seat. Hoping that she would not enter conversation, their fellow passenger talked non-stop to Sydney about the world's problems and the dysfunctional Labor Party that was wrecking Australia. The woman obviously had no idea that neither Dee nor Priscilla had even an inkling of what was happening in Australia, never mind the world, so they simply nodded in agreement and were deprived of any sleep.

When the plane landed in Sydney and with no baggage to *claim, they anxiously caught a taxi home. What state would it be in? Did it even still exist?* On arrival it appeared exactly how they had left it.

Priscilla went next door to see if her late father's old friend had collected any mail for her. She knew that the power and phone would have long ago been cut off. Dee tried the car battery but of course it was dead.

Seven months later, Dee and Priscilla, at long last caught up with their former lives. Accounts were paid, new drivers' licences obtained, new bank cards and having to adapt to the everyday life in a modern society. They envied the life of the Stone People who did not have to deal with all the bureaucracy and red tape that blocked their paths. Modern society was just a minefield of thousands of autocrats trying to justify the unjustifiable.

****

A year passed and Priscilla sat languidly on the deck of their yacht, watching Dee catch the evening meal. They had been at sea for six weeks and this was their first stop at an uninhabited island off the Queensland coast. Priscilla had been lucky in that, even in a slow market, the home her father had left her sold easily and as soon as they could, they sailed out of Sydney Harbour the following week. Priscilla packed her father's documents and her photos and story, leaving them with the family solicitors to be sent to the university on her death.

They gave their furniture to St Vinnies along with wardrobes full of clothes. Priscilla smiled as she looked at Dee clad only in a pair of tattered shorts. Priscilla wore absolutely nothing, basking in the afternoon sun, free at last and the oceans of the world waiting.

Dee glanced over at Priscilla who looked totally relaxed, sporting only a pair of sunglasses.

'Looking good there old girl,' he laughed cheekily.

'Still a bullshitter Dee my love. I think you need glasses; wrinkled skin, saggy tits; I look shit,' laughed Priscilla.

'After what we survived, it's no wonder we look so decrepit!' replied Dee.

'You know what Dee; I reckon it was the best lesson I ever learnt in my life. The Stone People taught me that our consumerist life is unsustainable. They have lived in the escarpment for centuries and survived without upsetting the environment, yet *we* have inhabited Australia for a mere two hundred years and if we keep going, will destroy it in the *next* two hundred!' commented Priscilla passionately.

'Unfortunately my darling, they will soon no longer exist. Already they have reached an unsustainable level, even foregoing their traditional ceremonies, simply I suppose, because of the small number but humanity and the planet will continue to evolve, change, no matter what. How fortunate are we though, to have had the finances to escape the world our generation created; so many are trapped,' commented

Dee frowning deeply.

'I suppose what Dad was trying to prove basically means nothing now anyhow. He was right; I'm sure that several migrations *did* occur but does it really matter? George and Mary and the rest of Indigenous Australia will have to go on trying to live together with the rest of Australia. Multiculturalism will create a far different landscape for us all so Dee, as a couple of old drop-outs, I sincerely hope we have many years to enjoy each other's company and sail together. This planet of ours is all we have, and it is so beautiful despite what mankind is doing to it so let's just make the most of it,' said Priscilla rather philosophically as she went to prepare dinner.

Dee stood watching the orange sunset and agreed with Priscilla that it truly is a wonderful and unique planet. Like Priscilla, he too regarded his time with the Stone People as one of the greatest periods of his life; the only downside being their inability to readapt to modern everyday life.

Dee felt humbled that he was able to sail away while so many parts of society struggled to keep up with spiralling costs and regulation inhibiting all aspects of daily life. He so cherished the lifestyle of the Stone People; their uncomplicated day-to-day survival, their ability to accept everything without complaint and the selflessness of the aged and infirm who refused to be a burden on the rest of the group. They shared everything and owned nothing. It belonged to all and each one faced death with a dignity that he now appreciated as being one of honour; not wanting to live if incapable of contributing to their clan.

Priscilla appeared from the galley wrapped in a soft, pink sarong carrying a tray with two glasses of wine and nibbles. 'Yes,' thought Dee, 'life has been great. I've found my true love and experienced an adventure few will ever have the privilege and all thanks to a whim several years ago to catch up with an old colleague for a few drinks and chat about the "old times".

'Yep,' he smiled, 'some decisions turn out to be the right ones.'